THE DONN, TX

COLLECTION VOL. 1

1952

1969

1865

1926

BY

ERIC BUTLER

Naked Cat Press

For information contact:
Naked Cat Press
http://www.nakedcatpress.com
edbutler17@gmail.com

Book design by Naked Cat Press

Cover design by Don Noble of Rooster Republic Press

Edited by Lisa Lee

ISBN:978-1-7341795-5-2

First Edition: November 2021
    10 9 8 7 6 5 4 3 2 1

TO JOHN,

BROTHERS HUG.

THE IDEA OF DONN, TX CAME ABOUT IN THE SUMMER OF 2021.

THAT IDEA BECAME THE SHORT STORY DONN, TX 1952, WHICH I'VE INCLUDED HERE.

WITH JUST FOUR WORDS, A NEW WORLD OF HORROR WAS BORN.

SOMEWHERE IN TEXAS, 1952 ...

"Jerry, pull over," Debbie said with a groan.

"Not again," he growled but came to a stop on the side of the road.

She fumbled with the handle as her stomach clenched. Sweat ran down her face, stinging her eyes. Debbie tumbled out as the door swung open. She crawled away from the car, the sand hot to the touch, until she made it to the dying grass. Her stomach heaved as her fingers clenched at the ground.

The dry wind blew the stench back towards her, forcing her stomach to heave once again. A sense of relief washed over her as nothing else came up. Jerry's hand rested on her shoulder. She patted it, thankful he was with her.

"Okay?"

She nodded, afraid speaking may cause another wave. His hands slipped under her arms, lifting her to her feet and holding on until she offered another nod. He stepped to the passenger door of the car, then returned to her with an open bottle. Debbie grabbed it, filling her mouth with the warm liquid before swishing it around and spitting it out.

"Thanks," she murmured, her stomach settling down.

"Maybe we should stop now," he suggested, pointing to the top of the rise. "I see a motel sign. We could get some sleep, and hopefully, you'll feel better."

Debbie bit her bottom lip. She was anxious to get to her mother, but the doctor did say she had a few weeks left. She glanced at Jerry and sighed. His worry was plain. Reaching to place her hand on his cheek, she offered him a grateful smile.

"Okay, honey," she said. "Some stationary rest might just do the trick."

He led her to the car and helped her in before hurrying to his side and pulling back onto the lonely road.

* * *

"So do you think it's open?" Jerry asked as they pulled into the parking lot.

The motel was a simple one-story structure. He counted nine doors, but he was pretty sure only six or seven led to actual rooms. *Only need one.* He tapped the steering wheel, studying for any signs of life.

"Oh God," Debbie mumbled, her left hand coming up to cover her lips as her right gripped the handle.

Jerry sighed as his wife scrambled from the car and began vomiting again. *Last time I agree to stop at just any roadside diner.* He slid out and started around the car.

Debbie held up her arm, waving him off.

"Okay... I'll go check if anyone is here," he called out as he hurried to the first door.

Jerry paused, his hand holding the doorknob. He stared at the sign in the small window to the side. The sign itself was dark black, but it was the words that held his attention. *Welcome weary traveler. Your journey nears its end.* He studied the red letters a moment before shaking his head. *God, I wish.* They'd only been on the road a day, and he expected, after this break, it would be another day before they arrived at Debbie's mother's house. *That's when the fun really begins.*

Jerry turned the knob and entered.

Debbie leaned against the car. The sun beat down on her, but she welcomed the distraction. At some point, she assumed her stomach would simply run out of contents. *Hope it's soon.* She studied the door Jerry left open but couldn't make out anything past the frame. Debbie crossed her fingers. *Please have clean sheets and running water.* A cold shower was just what she needed.

A loud caw grabbed her attention, and she glanced around. Three of the largest crows she'd ever seen stood on the arm of a scarecrow across the street. Debbie stood straight, shielding her eyes to see clearer. The crows hopped around the scarecrow, moving from arm to arm, occasionally resting on its head. They turned to stare at her, offering more cries as if calling her over.

The scarecrow was on a pole towering over the cornstalks that filled the field across the way. It wore all black, bits of graying hay sticking out at the collar and waist. A burlap sack covered the place its head would be; shiny black eyes sparkled in the sunlight. *Are those onyx?*

Debbie shuffled towards the road, pausing long enough to check both ways before continuing to the other side. The crows grew agitated, hopping up and down and crying at her approach. She paused, hesitant to leave the safety of the road. She stood on the shoulder and shielded her eyes once again.

The crows settled down, returning her stare. A chill ran through Debbie, causing her to shiver. The largest crow jumped into the air, spread its wings, and floated to the ground. It landed in front of her and clawed at the ground. Dry laughter floated on the wind. Debbie's head snapped up, searching through the corn to find the owner. Her eyes fell on the scarecrow and froze.

Its head was turned, both dark eyes locked on her face. A wicked smile decorated the burlap skin as the laughter grew in volume. A sharp jab of pain tore through Debbie's leg, and she looked down with a gasp. Blood glistened on the crow's beak as it moved to peck at her once again.

Her foot slammed out, connecting with the bird and sending black feathers into the air.

Debbie spun to run back to the car when an eighteen-wheeler rushed past, its horn blaring a warning. She stumbled back, losing her balance and tumbling to the hard-packed soil. Blinking against the dying sunlight, Debbie struggled to raise her hands as a shadow passed above her. The laughter began anew as the crow landed on her chest with a caw. A sob slipped from her lips as she watched her blood drip from the beast's beak.

Jerry stood in the lobby. There was a counter splitting the room in half, and on his side was a coffee table and two dusty chairs upholstered in a flowery pattern he vaguely remembered his Grandmother having years ago. A few issues of *Life* sat on the table, and he made a note to see if the owner was okay with him taking them back to the room. *Debbie may need some rest, but I'm wide awake.*

The counter was bare except for a dull metal bell. Next to a curtain of dark fabric, a cubbyhole box decorated the back wall with eight open spots, though only six were numbered. Glancing around, Jerry hoped the actual rooms' upkeep was better than the lobby, but he doubted it. *Beggars can't be choosers.*

Stepping closer, he popped his hand down on the button, happy to find it at least worked. He waited a moment before striking the bell again and glanced back at the door. *I hope Debbie is okay.*

"Help ya?" a voice called out.

With a start, Jerry returned his attention to the counter. He placed his hand on his chest as he forced a smile on his lips. "Wowzers, you really gave me a scare. I need a room...just for the night."

The man was beyond old. The only word that Jerry could make fit was *ancient. How is this guy still up and about?* The motel manager seemed to be bending in on himself, and Jerry thought he might have been extremely tall when he stood straight. *Whenever that might have been.* His skin was paper-thin and stained an off-yellow color, and there was no evidence of muscles or fat on his body.

The man reached down and, after a moment, heaved an oversized book onto the counter with a bang. He opened it to the center and began to flip the pages until he arrived at the first blank one. Spinning the book, he produced a pen and held it out for Jerry.

"A night is going to cost you ten dollars," he said in a raspy whisper.

"Ten dollars?" Jerry asked, the pen stopping in mid-stroke.

"Y'all are more than welcome to continue on, but there ain't another place out here for quite a while. Dinner is included, if it helps."

Jerry released the breath he held in an exaggerated sigh. *I guess dinner does help.* He finished filling out the book and reached into his back pocket to pull out his wallet. He counted out ten dollars and laid it on the counter next to the book. The old man offered a toothless smile, and Jerry began to wonder just what passed for dinner in these parts.

He opened his mouth to ask when Debbie's cries sounded from outside. He turned to rush out when the old man called out, "Room 3 ... door's unlocked."

Jerry nodded his thanks and hurried out to the parking lot. He spun around, searching for Debbie when he realized she wasn't by the car, and froze when his eyes hit the scarecrow across the road. The two outsized crows sitting on its left arm glanced at Jerry before returning their attention to the ground. A chill rushed through him, forcing the Texas heat from his body.

The scarecrow's head was angled as if it studied the ground with wide black eyes, which sparkled in a way that made Jerry think of excitement. His stomach clenched when he noticed the large grin stitched on the burlap face.

"Debbie?!" he called out as he started to run across the road.

A wordless cry answered him, and then the crows began to imitate it with their caws. He skidded to a stop as he left the road and found Debbie on her back, her bloody arms between her face and a third crow attempting to peck her eyes out. Between failed attempts, it cried in frustration.

Jerry rushed forward, kicking out and striking the bird with the point of his shoe.

"Get!" he cried, waving his arms to scare the crows away.

The two on the scarecrow sat unimpressed as they waited for the third to land on the opposite arm. It let loose a violent cry of displeasure before pecking its beak against the scarecrow's open mouth. Jerry bent over and picked Debbie up, pulling her tight to his chest. He glared at the scarecrow before turning to carry his wife to the motel.

"You really suck at your job, pal," he called over his shoulder.

His only answer was the cries of the crows.

Bastards are laughing at us. He shook his head, turning to look once more at the group when he was safely on the other side of the road. Jerry's stomach dropped as they locked eyes and he realized the scarecrow now stared straight ahead.

The door swung open, and Jerry carried Debbie to the closest twin bed to set her down. He gently took her arms and held them straight, inspecting the damage the bird's beak had inflicted. Her skin was torn and slashed in a number of spots, but nothing appeared too deep. He moved to her leg and let out a hiss as he studied the wound there.

Debbie's sobs shook her body as Jerry finished his inspection. She kept her head down as if afraid to make eye contact. He slipped his finger under her chin and raised her head, then kissed her on the forehead and stepped back.

"I'm going to see if that old man has a first-aid kit. Sit tight."

She offered a slight nod and laid back onto the bed. He slipped out, closing the door behind him. Rushing back to the front desk, he glanced at the corn. The scarecrow watched him with dead, black eyes.

What did you expect...it'd be gone?

Jerry spat in its direction and shook his head. *Trip is messing with my head.* He gripped the knob and pushed the door open, hurrying to the counter to ring the bell. After the third attempt grew quiet, the man appeared from behind the curtain.

"Help ya?"

"I need a first aid kit...maybe some booze?" Jerry asked as he stared at the old man. After a moment of silence, he added, "Some damn crows attacked my wife...over by that fucking scarecrow."

The old man grew still. His eyes locked onto Jerry's face, and a smile crept upon his lips before he whispered, "Did it taste her blood?"

"Excuse me?" Jerry asked, his voice growing hot as he reached over and grabbed the man by his collar. "What the hell does that even mean? Yes, a bird cut my wife, and I need your help. Now!"

"Oh, well, if it was just the bird..." the old man trailed off as he turned to shuffle back through the curtain.

Jerry stood there a moment, his hands balled into tight fists. He glanced at the parking lot, noting the creeping shadows as the sun began to set. *I don't have time for this.* He hopped onto the counter and slipped down the other side. Pushing back the curtain, he rushed forward ...

And slammed into a wall.

Jerry stumbled back, his head striking the counter as he fell to the carpeted floor. Darkness overtook him as his final thought faded. *Where did that come from?*

Jerry's eyes opened to darkness. A single beam of light shined upon the number three on the cubbyhole. He groaned as he sat up, his hand cupping the back of his head. It came away damp, and he wondered if it was as bad as it felt. Struggling to stand, he used the counter to pull himself to his feet.

Stars flashed before him as Jerry struggled to stay upright. Clenching his eyes closed, he took a few deep breaths. His eyes reopened as he exhaled the last one.

Debbie.

He struggled to slide over the counter and get to the front door. He paused as he stared out across the parking lot.

Even with the moonlight, the property was mostly shadows. *How long was I out?* He hoped Debbie fell asleep, but worry began to grow in the pit of his stomach. Stepping out, he paused as a loud caw sounded from across the street. Laughter floated on the breeze, and his blood froze. *Is the old man out here?*

Jerry stumbled towards room three, his legs wobbling and refusing to move any faster than a shuffle. The laughter built in volume until it drowned out everything. Jerry slammed his hands over his ears, hoping to block out the raspy, uneven flow of glee.

Soft light shined around the door, and he called out Debbie's name. He tried again, wondering if he was speaking louder than the laughter. He took a deep breath to really belt it out when the door swung open. The laughter died suddenly, and an eerie calm washed over Jerry. His hands slipped down to his side as he stepped closer to the room. The only sounds were the crunch of gravel under his steps and the pounding of his heart.

As Jerry stepped to the doorway, he paused, unable to process the scene in room three. His eyes slammed shut as a low moan of anguish slipped past his lips. He tumbled down, no longer able to find the strength to stand as images of what he'd seen flashed through his head. Debbie's clothes littered the floor, while Debbie herself lay on the bed, her legs spread open as if seductively enticing him to slip between them. Her mouth was frozen open in a wordless howl of torment, and her flayed skin now hung haphazardly over the two lamps in the room. The hot white light muted by the bloody tissue set the mood as she had on their wedding night.

"It's the little details that make nights like this so special," a raspy, dry voice whispered from behind as rough fingers gripped Jerry's hair and pulled his head back.

Razor-sharp pain bloomed across Jerry's throat as the laughter began anew.

Jerry's eyes fluttered open to the sound of a bell dinging. He shook his head, hoping to remove the cobwebs that were leaving him so groggy and confused. His skin began to tingle as the bell sounded again. *Ding.* He stood, his arms outstretched as he stumbled through the dark towards the sound. *Ding.*

Light seared away the darkness, leaving Jerry's vision blurred. With each blink, more came into focus. A man stood on the other side of a counter. *No, not a counter* ... the *counter.* Jerry glanced around, taking in the cubbyhole boxes and the curtain before refocusing on the man.

"Yes, hello, I need a room for the night," he said in a clipped, fast-paced tone.

Jerry stared at him a moment before reaching under the counter. The oversized book felt natural in his hands, and he hesitated, relishing the weight, then placed the book on the counter. He opened it to the middle and began to flip until he found the first blank page. Spinning the book for the man, he produced a pen and offered a smile.

"You're in luck, we just had a room open up."

SOMEWHERE IN TEXAS, 1969 ...

CHAPTER ONE

"How is every road in this Godforsaken place under construction?" Frank asked as he followed the detour signs to yet another country road.

"Too bad we left the highway," Jane said, forcing a straight face when he glanced in her direction. She winced when a snicker came from the back seat.

Frank studied the rearview mirror a moment before letting out a big sigh. *Damn it...she's not wrong.* Frank reached over and patted Jane's knee. She hesitated, then grabbed his hand and offered a squeeze. It was taking some time, but she seemed to be coming around to his being home. A year out in the jungle changed him more than he cared to admit.

"I can't help being hungry," he said, forcing a laugh that wasn't really there. "How could I have ever known we'd never get back on I-45?"

"Since you've been home, you're always hungry," a voice said from the back, followed by more snickers and giggles.

Frank let loose another sigh but kept quiet. *How did I get talked into driving these two bitches to Houston?* He glanced back at the rearview mirror, a sneer on his lips. The two girls in the back grew quiet. He stared until they dropped their heads, cutting off their line of sight.

Goddamn right. He bit his bottom lip to keep the words from tumbling out. He survived Charlie for months; it would be a cold day in Hell before he surrendered to a couple of high school seniors.

Jane pulled her hand free and smacked his arm hard enough to cause him to wince.

He dropped his vision back to the road, his jaw clenched in silent frustration. *You're going to blow it before we even make it to Rice. Cool it, Frank.*

"Shit...sorry," he mumbled as he gripped the wheel with both hands, his knuckles turning white from the pressure.

They drove on in silence, the tension building.

Jane reached to the dashboard to click on the radio. Three pops sounded as she turned the knob. The radio powered up, but only static played. Frank's mind wandered to the pops. They were such a familiar sound, but he was struggling to place it.

A vision of the jungle flashed through his head.

Frank stopped breathing. The static from the radio morphed into the buzz of the jungle, drowning his senses in a steady hiss.

Jane gripped the knob and rolled the dial over the numbers until a blast of music filled the car.

"Frank?" Jane asked, concern evident in her voice.

Her hand rested on his shoulder. He wanted to look, to see her touching him, but instead, he continued to stare straight ahead. The static in his head grew in volume, drowning out the sounds of the car moving over the uneven country road and the voice of Johnny Cash coming through the speakers. Jane pushed on his arm, looking for any reaction. He smirked. *Take more than that to move this soldier.*

An ache filled his chest, the kind of ache he got traipsing around the bush when all he wanted was to be home. *To be home with Jane.* His face began to darken, and he wondered if there was any reason he wasn't breathing. Screams began to filter through the roar in his head. His vision darkened as helplessness washed over him.

At least my last breath is here, in Texas...

CHAPTER TWO

Jane woke to the screech of the car horn. She flinched in pain as she struggled to push back from the dashboard. *What the hell happened?* She blinked back the pain as she tried to figure out if she meant to the car or Frank. She'd seen him freeze once before right when he got back, but she'd chalked it up to the fireworks at the end of the game. This was different, though.

"Frank?" she asked before forcing her eyes to focus through the haze.

His face was pressed against the steering wheel, blood running from a gash on his forehead. Jane gripped his shoulder and pulled him back, grateful for the sudden silence. A moan from the back pulled her attention away from Frank. The girls slumped against each other, arms and legs tangled together. *No blood, thankfully.*

"Is everyone okay?" she asked, her voice thick with pain.

Am I okay?

"I think so."

Jane's eyes squinted as she stared at the girls. *Was that Mary?* For some reason, she thought if it was her sister, everything would be all right. She realized she was holding her breath as Frank had before the crash. It came out in a rush as she reached back to grab Mary's hand.

"What happened?" Mary's best friend, Cindy, asked as her eyes fluttered open.

"I don't know, but Frank is hurt," Jane said. She squeezed Mary's hand before letting go. "Are ya sure y'all are okay?"

"Yeah," Cindy replied after a moment. The girls untangled and opened their doors to slip out of the car.

Jane returned her attention to Frank, relieved to see his chest rise and fall in a shallow but steady rhythm. She popped open the glove box and pulled out the first aid kit and a bandanna. *This seems like a lot of blood.* She wiped away the excess to expose a nasty cut. Fumbling through the kit, she let out a grunt of frustration. *Where are they?*

"Yes," she exclaimed as she pulled out an iodine swab.

Frank's eyes shot open as she pressed it to his forehead, his hand grabbing her wrist and pulling her arm down.

"Damn it, Frank," she cried out, surprise quickly turning to fear as his fingers tightened. "Let go...you're hurting me!"

"Jane? You can't be out in the bush...you're my only anchor to real life," he mumbled through clenched teeth before slumping back.

"We have a problem," Cindy called out.

No shit. Jane stared at Frank a moment longer before sliding out. The car was stopped a few feet from the road, the front bent around a thick tree trunk. She hurried around the back to see what the two girls were staring at. Both tires on the driver's side were flat, but it was the jagged hole in the driver's door that held their attention.

"Is that...a bullet hole?" she asked, already sure of the answer.

Two flats and they were in the middle of nowhere. She glanced at the girls and forced a smile on her lips as she reached out and pulled them closer.

"Ladies, I need you guys to focus," Jane said, trying to keep her voice as light as possible. *Having two frightened eighteen-year-olds will not make this easier.* "Frank is hurt, but I think once he's oriented, he'll be fine. We need to find help. A little way back, I think there was a sign for a motel somewhere out here. If we're lucky, it's on this road."

"Yeah," Mary said with a shaky voice as she stared at Frank's unconscious form. "But what if he isn't?"

Jane reached out and pressed her hand against her sister's face. "If he can't move, well, someone will need to stay with him while the others go for help."

"No-no-no-no," Cindy began to repeat, her eyes shiny with unshed tears.

"Stop it," Jane snapped as she gripped her sister's friend by the shoulder and began to shake her. "We don't have a choice. Y'all aren't children anymore. Now get a hold of yourself."

Mary pushed through her sister's grip and pulled Cindy tight against her. Jane turned from them and opened the driver's door. She noticed a hole in the seat, just under his leg, and let out a gasp. *Lucky break there.* She reached over Frank, grabbing the kit so she could try again to clean up the nasty gash on his forehead. He let out a moan as the swab pressed against the wound, but this time he made no motion to wake up.

Jane finished taping up the bandage and stepped back. She glanced at the sky. *Might be a couple of hours left before it grows dark.* The last thing she wanted was for them to be separated after nightfall. Sighing, she turned to break the news to the girls.

Mary held up her hand as she continued to whisper into Cindy's ear. After a moment of silence, Cindy offered a slight nod, and Mary pulled away from her friend.

"Okay, we'll go," she said as she stared at Jane. "If something is wrong, he has the best chance with you here. We'll find the motel and bring back help."

Jane offered a sad smile. She couldn't argue as Mary's points were exactly the ones Jane prepared to make, but her little sister was growing up too fast. Jane was in her third year of nursing school, but more importantly, if he woke up confused like before, she was the only one with any hope of calming him down.

"Hold on," she said, and she moved back to her side of the car to grab the flashlight she had seen earlier in the glove box. "Take this in case it gets dark."

Mary grabbed it with a nod, then reached out her free hand to Cindy, who hesitated a moment before taking it with a sigh. The two began to walk away from the car, their speed increasing as Mary pulled her friend along.

God, please keep them safe. It was the prayer she'd started using when Frank left for Vietnam. It got him home; she hoped it kept the girls out of harm's way as well.

CHAPTER THREE

"I told you that was too soon," Harold Smite said with a huff.

He pulled the binoculars down and glared at the man to his left. Jim Brooks only shrugged and packed up his Remington Model 700.

"You wanted the car disabled," he said before spitting out a string of tobacco juice. "It's disabled. I'd rather not get any closer."

"Almost a mile from the damned target zone," Harold said through a clenched jaw. "You better hope this works, or we might not have a choice on how close we get."

"Jesus, it's hot," Cindy whined. She twirled her hair with her free hand and held it up and away from her neck.

"Sorry," Mary said.

Cindy glanced at her and forced a smile to her lips. "You didn't make it hot, silly."

Mary glanced at her, then returned her attention to the blacktop they strolled on. Neither was willing to admit just why Mary was sorry. They should already be in Houston, some cute guys showing them around Rice to see the campus up close. Instead, they were sweating their asses off God-knows-where.

Cindy squeezed Mary's hand before pulling her closer to offer her a hug. After three steps, sobs began to wrack through Cindy's body. The women sank to the ground, and she buried her face into Mary's shoulder while her friend stroked her hair and offered soothing noises.

Mary let a few moments pass before speaking. "Cindy, sweetie, I know thinking a car might come along would be a blessing, but we are sitting in the middle of the only road."

Cindy pulled back, her eyes puffy and red, but a smile split her face. "Yeah, that would suck."

Mary returned the smile, pulling her friend to her feet as she stood. They started to walk again, no longer holding hands. Cindy stepped off the blacktop to search for some shade from the occasional tree. On the opposite side, corn stalks swayed in the hot breeze.

"Shouldn't these be gone?" Mary called out as she studied the cornfields.

"Yeah, today is the last day of harvest...might do things differently here, though," Cindy said without looking.

Mary nodded slowly. Cindy would know, her family owned most of the farmland in Motley County. A loud caw broke into her thoughts. She pulled up and stared at the largest crow she'd ever seen standing in the middle of the road.

"Cindy," she hissed in warning when her friend continued to move forward.

"Huh?" Cindy mumbled, glancing at Mary and then following her eyes to spot the bird.

It hopped back and forth as if the blacktop was burning its feet in front of the remains of an indistinguishable animal. It paused, pecked down at the lump of meat, then returned to its strange dance.

Mary gasped in horror at the carcass's eye resting in the crow's beak.

"Oh, gross," Cindy exclaimed, stumbling back to hide behind Mary, sandwiching her right hand between both of her friend's.

The crow turned its head, studying the two for a moment before clamping its beak shut. Gore squished from the eyeball and dripped to the blacktop. Cindy began to gag, moving her free hand to her mouth. Mary stepped back to stand even with her friend.

The crow's head twisted back and forth, its eye never leaving them.

Maybe we should just head back. Mary glanced over her shoulder; a tiny groan slipped out. Five oversized crows formed a line to block the road back. Each bird kept one eye on the girls as they all hopped forward in unison.

"What the fuck?" Cindy cried out when she followed Mary's line of sight.

Mary squeezed her hand and shushed her. The last thing they needed was to startle these creatures. She glanced at Cindy and tried to smile.

"Honey, we need to get out of the open," she whispered, tugging her friend closer. "When I say go, we need to run to the corn. If we're lucky, we get there unscathed and these things grow bored and leave."

She didn't want to give voice to what would happen if that many birds got a hold of them out here. *Make that pile of roadkill look like a good time.* The birds began to issue random cries as they grew closer. *Now or never...*

"Go."

The two girls sprang towards the corn. Cindy stumbled a moment, but Mary used newfound strength to keep her on her feet as they ran towards cover. The crows let out their caws simultaneously, drowning out all other sound as they took to the sky. They blocked out the sun, plunging the girls into shadow.

Tears streamed down Mary's face as they sprinted closer to the corn. *Please God, let me be fast enough this time.* As they left the road, a cloud of dust rose around them.

The birds' cries increased, reflecting their rage and frustration.

A wave of relief washed over Mary. *Almost there.* She glanced back to offer Cindy encouragement, but the words froze as the crows swooped down to seize Cindy by the shoulders and lift her from the ground.

Mary tumbled to the ground as Cindy was ripped from her grip, her cries drowning out the crows' excitement. Mary rolled to the edge of the corn, horrified to watch her friend rise into the air but unable to tear her eyes away.

"Help," Cindy cried out before returning to the wordless howls of terror from before. Her legs flailed in the empty space, her body twisting and turning as the crows dragged her higher and higher.

A puff of dust pulled Mary's attention from her friend. The original crow studied her, blood still dripping from its beak. She reached back, her fingers curling around the flashlight sticking up from her back pocket.

"What do you want?" she asked, her voice barely above a whisper.

The crow remained silent while the cries of the others moved farther away. Mary knew she was running out of time. *Batter's up, champ.* She reared back, suddenly resting on her knees, as the crow sprang towards her.

Mary swung the flashlight and was rewarded with a startled caw and a burst of feathers as it crushed into the bird's head. She crawled into the cornfield, struggling to her feet, then running in the direction she last saw Cindy and the crows.

CHAPTER FOUR

"Do you hear that?" Jane said, not expecting an answer.

Frank lay motionless, the shallow rise and fall of his chest the only evidence he was still alive. Checking the dashboard clock, Jane wondered if the girls might still be close enough to be heard. *God, I hope not.*

Even with the doors wide open, the car was still an oven in the shade. Jane slipped out and walked a few feet away from the car. Glancing back, she wondered if she should wake him. *At least move him out of that hot box.* She shuddered at the thought as it reminded her of the stories he told of the war. Shaking her head, she forced her attention back towards the direction the girls went.

She held her breath and strained to pick up the noise again, but there was nothing but the buzz of insects and the faraway cries of some crows. Sighing, she turned back to the car.

"Well, Frank, gonna need ya to wake the fuck up," she said, walking back and kicking at the ground with each word.

They were supposed to be in Houston, having their honeymoon while the girls hung out on the campus. Her skin flushed in excitement as she imagined their lips pressed together while his hands slid over her smooth skin and slipped into her panties.

Jane sighed, shaking her head to break the fantasy. *Damn it, Frank.* He hadn't touched her since he'd returned home, at least not that way, and it left her frustrated; frustrated and confused. She hurried to the driver's side and studied her husband.

The boy she knew growing up no longer existed. He liked to joke that the heat over there melted that away, but she knew it was something worse. Jane saw it clearly anytime he accidentally made eye contact. Something haunted him, and it was always there. This trip was going to be the beginning of the process of healing him, at least that had been her hope. *Fat chance now.*

Jane froze. It wasn't the sudden quiet that unnerved her but the fact that Frank's eyes were open and staring past her. Danger and raw emotion sparkled through his green eyes in a way she'd never seen before.

Frank swung his legs out slowly, his hands on the doorframe for balance. Jane began to shake, but her head refused to turn. She kept her eyes on Frank, hopeful he'd be able to do something in his state.

"Jane, hon," he said in a way that might have sounded calm to anyone but her. The fear in his voice soaked into her being, and she wondered if she could make her legs respond. When she did not move, he barked, "Now."

With a jerk, she stumbled towards him as he stood by the car. He wrapped his arm around her shoulder and offered a hug. She fought the urge to bury her face into his shoulder and turned to see what spooked him.

"God damn it," she growled, punching him in the side. There wasn't anything there. "You scared me half to death."

He winced at her blow but kept his arm around her. His eyes swept back and forth. His free arm rose, extending his finger towards the other side of the road and the stalks that were swaying in the breeze.

"There's something there... watching us," he whispered. "Where are the girls?"

"They went ahead for help while you slept. You have a nasty head injury."

He fingered the bandage on his forehead before offering a nod, then grabbed the keys, closed the door, and shuffled to the other side. He popped open the glove box and searched a moment before Jane explained where the flashlight was.

Frank held still a moment, then sighed and flashed a smile. "That was good. I'm sure this is nothing. Just feel better if we were together. I'm okay to walk, and we need to catch up with them."

Jane stared at him; the smile was nothing more than to disarm her. After all these years, he was incapable of hiding his true thoughts. *Well, except whatever happened over this last year...those thoughts are still in his head and eating him alive.*

Frank began to shuffle away from the car, gaining more confidence with each step until he was marching. Jane let out a squeak of surprise as she realized he was leaving her behind with her thoughts. Rushing forward, she caught up and slipped next to him on the left. He reached over and guided her to the other side, slipping her hand into his, his eyes studying the corn the entire time.

"Did it follow me home?" Frank said, so softly that Jane thought she imagined it until he repeated the words.

CHAPTER FIVE

Mary ran through the corn stalks. Cindy's cries grew fainter, but she couldn't be sure if it was due to distance, exhaustion, or shock. She rushed over the uneven ground, her breaths coming in large gasps. Sweat soaked through her t-shirt, yet she wished she had long sleeves for added protection as the stalks whipped at her from each side.

A sudden scream of terror echoed through the field, bringing Mary to a halt. A hot, dusty breeze moved through the corn, but the only thing she could hear was the pounding of her heart. She turned slowly, making a complete circle, as she searched for any sign of movement other than the gentle sway of the corn.

Mary ran the back of her hand against her forehead as sweat stung her eyes. She gasped when she noticed large smears of blood decorating the back of her hand. The liquid ran freely from a multitude of cuts on her arm, dripping from her fingertips to the parched soil. Another scream pulled Mary's attention away from her injuries. *Worry about it later.* She started forward, moving in the direction she believed the scream came from. *Hold on, Cindy, I'm coming.*

The dry ground behind her shifted and quaked, soaking up the spilled blood. Moments later, a hand shoved upwards, breaking the surface.

CHAPTER SIX

Jerry stood behind the counter. He wanted to enjoy the summer heat since it was the last day before he sank back into the darkness. Oh, he might make an appearance in a few months when the barrier was weaker, but that was never guaranteed. Plus it lacked the punch of summer. *Nothing like the sweet kiss of Texas in July.*

Of course, if they missed their quota, he and the others would be visited with what seemed an eternity of pain. *Better to make it.* He worked hard to ensure that didn't happen again. After the debacle of '53, he finally learned exactly what the price of failure was; more importantly, Jerry learned exactly what they expected from him.

The door opened and closed. A man dressed in a uniform stood in the lobby and glanced around, then stepped to the counter and popped his hand down on the bell. *Ding.* The sound resonated through Jerry, who closed his eyes. *Ding.* He wasn't sure, but the sensation was much worse when he was in the light. *Ding.* A bird flew into the window with a crunch, drawing the attention of the uniformed man.

"This can't be good, Sheriff Smite," Jerry said to the man's back.

"Jesus," he said with a jolt. "How'd you get up front so quick? Never mind, I think it's good news. There are four people on the property."

Jerry raised an eyebrow, staring silently at the man, who pulled his hat off his head, running the brim through his fingers as he rocked back and forth a bit.

"Well, heading this way at least. We lost sight of two of them, but there's a couple walking on the blacktop. Can't be more than ten, fifteen minutes away from the border."

"We can only pray, but remember what happened the last time we fell short..." Jerry trailed off, his eyes locked with the Sheriff's, who, after a moment, swallowed.

"No call for that," he whispered. "If these four don't work, I'll bring you more. We still have until midnight?"

Jerry nodded, then offered a grin. "Best bet for you and yours is completing this job earlier than later. I can't always call the monsters back once they've been released."

The Sheriff stepped away from the counter, walking backward, his eyes glued on Jerry the whole time. He stopped before running into the wall and reached over to open the door.

"Good luck, Harold," Jerry called out as the man stepped through the doorway. "I'll be rooting for ya."

CHAPTER SEVEN

"You'd think we'd have come across them by now," Frank said, breaking the silence.

Jane nodded, her thoughts still on the last thing he had said. *What followed him home?* A burst of darkness flashed before her, and she let out a cry of surprise and stumbled backward. Frank pulled her closer, using his body as a shield as the darkness swooped back towards them.

"What is wrong with this crow?" Frank asked as he swung his free arm at the bird.

Jane whimpered, her eyes locked onto the bird as it fluttered to the ground. The left side of its head was caved in, with bits of brain and blood exposed against the dark feathers. *How is it alive, let alone flying?* She shuddered as the bird opened its beak wide, issuing a number of ear-piercing cries.

They watched the bird as it stumbled around, one eye always facing their direction, until it slumped to the ground with a final cry of frustration. A stiff breeze flowed over the corn, blowing dust into their faces. Frank sputtered, and he turned to shield Jane as more of the grime blew towards them.

The wind howled like a beast, growing in volume and forcing them to cover their ears. The cornstalks rocked back and forth as the wind came together in a funnel of dirt and crud spinning over the crow's carcass.

Jane cracked her eyes, mesmerized by the twirling muck as it swirled over the dead bird. The funnel grew tighter as it drew closer to the blacktop.

A hush fell over Jane and Frank, the wind's cry no longer audible. The wind continued to blow as the funnel spun faster and faster. Jane's eyes popped open as she struggled to understand what she was witnessing. The tunnel began to expand, pushing outward while its tip stayed tight over the motionless bird. The shape of a man took form in the swirling madness, first kneeling but soon standing.

An unheard gasp slipped from her lips, and she clung tightly to Frank as waves of fear washed over her body. The man turned his attention to them, lifting his arm until he pointed a single finger at Frank. The funnel suddenly drew in, blurring its grime with the shadowy form within. Jane realized she was holding her breath, but her body refused to respond to her mental cries as she stood frozen. The twirling mess slowed for a single moment and allowed Jane to see the man clearly. He wore deerskin pants and a shirt with long thin fringe, while black feathers hung loosely from his long dark hair.

Before she could make sense of what her eyes were viewing, an explosion tore the funnel apart. Sand tore across their bodies, scouring their skin. Frank spun, scooped Jane into his arms, and rushed towards the cornfield. He staggered from the force of the wind, which now seemed to follow their every step, and Jane worried they would fall before finding some cover.

Frank stepped from the road, slipping on the uneven earth. With an exclamation of surprise, he stumbled forward before losing his balance and dropping Jane to the ground. She rolled to the edge of the corn and curled up, hoping to gain some protection. She lost her breath as a sudden jerk pulled her from the ground. Opening her eyes a crack, she realized Frank carried her by her belt as the ground rushed by.

They crashed into the corn stalks, tumbling down to packed dirt. The howl of the wind increased once more until deafening. Jane watched the cloudless blue sky grow dark as the dust storm settled above the cornfield. Frank sat up, his eyes toward the sky, when the storm once again began to form a funnel. The tip stretched down past the tops of the stalks, growing thinner until it slammed into Frank's face. His lips parted with a scream of terror that was quickly cut short as it slipped into his mouth. The funnel spun faster until the whole thing disappeared into Frank.

An unsettling quiet fell upon the cornfield in the wake of the howling winds. Jane kept her eyes on Frank, who now was on all fours, gasping for breath. She crawled to him. He rocked back, resting on his knees as his fingers clawed at his throat. A strangled gurgle slipped past his lips as their eyes locked. Frank's eyes shone with unshed tears, but his face took on an expression of calm. His hands slipped to his lap as he mouthed *I love you.*

"No," she whispered, tears streaming down her face as grit streamed from his mouth.

It poured from him, scouring his insides until blood flowed from his open mouth to pool on the earth before him. The air rushed from him with a pop, and a splattering of blood sprayed out onto Jane. Frank teetered a moment, his eyes blank, then tumbled face-first into the bloody mud.

Jane stared at his body, her mouth agape as she tried to process what just happened. Her hand stretched toward Frank but froze when a breeze blew through the stalks, bringing dry, wheezing laughter to her ears.

"Best run," a voice suggested.

The stalks began to shudder and sway toward her. She crawled to Frank, checked his pulse. Deep sobs ripped from her chest as she moved her fingers around, hoping to find any signs of life. She wiped at her eyes and gasped. Standing a few feet away was the largest man she'd ever seen.

Besides being tall, the man was so wide he could almost be a square. She wouldn't describe the man as fat, for he carried the bulk well, yet she wondered if it would be qualified as muscle. His overalls were torn and filthy from God knows what. His feet were bare, as were his shoulders, but upon his head, he wore a loose burlap sack.

Upon the face, someone had stitched a broad mouth and cut two eye holes. But Jane saw nothing but darkness reflected there. She scrambled to her feet and stared at the stranger.

"I said run," the man said as he pulled a hatchet from his belt loop. "Ain't no fun if you don't."

CHAPTER EIGHT

Cindy slammed into the hard ground, knocking the breath from her lungs. Her shoulders ached from the gouges left by the crows' talons. Blood soaked into her shirt, causing it to stick to her skin. She struggled to rise, but something slammed into her back, driving her to the ground. One of the crow's eyes came into her peripheral vision. It studied her a moment before driving its beak into her shoulder.

Cindy cried out weakly before slumping into the dirt. Her body shook with silent sobs as she continued to fight for breath. The crow pulled back, its beak shiny with her blood. It released a cry and sprang into the sky. She rolled to her back, grateful for the shade that protected her from the setting sun.

The crow circled above, moving so lazily it seemed more a dream to Cindy. She followed its path until it flew out of her view. It issued another cry, pulling her attention behind her to a scarecrow suspended in the air on a thin platform. Its shiny black eyes seemed to be watching her lay on the ground.

Cindy struggled to her knees, her eyes locked on the stuffed man. The scarecrow wore all black with a tight burlap sack acting as its face. Someone had stitched a wide mouth in a crooked grin, giving those black eyes a sense of mischief that left Cindy unsettled.

The crow landed on the scarecrow's shoulder. It studied her a moment, then hopped closer to the head and smeared its beak against the stitched lips of the scarecrow. The stalks of corn began to sway as a strong wind blew through the cornfield. Cindy stared at the scarecrow, unable to break eye contact with the shiny black circles.

As the wind died down, Cindy realized she could hear laughter. It was soft, a weak, raspy noise, but it was building in strength as it went on. She glanced around, searching for the source. As the laughter grew louder, her eyes moved back to the scarecrow. *That's not possible...is it?*

The laughter stopped abruptly, leaving Cindy in absolute silence.

"Anything is possible with enough blood," the scarecrow said, its voice as dry as the earlier laughter.

Cindy began to scream as the scarecrow dropped from its perch.

CHAPTER NINE

Mary crept through the corn. There was laughter in the wind, and it filled her with dread. She shuddered at the thought of blindly running into someone out there. *Just find Cindy and make it back to the road.*

She scanned the tops of the corn, looking for any movement. Her eyes fell upon the upper body of a scarecrow. A chill rushed through her as she pulled up. It was looking directly at her. *Don't be silly.* But she was unable to pull her eyes away from the shiny black circles staring in her direction. The wind picked up, swaying the corn back and forth, and the laughter returned, gaining in volume, causing the hairs on Mary's neck to rise.

She glanced back, needing the confirmation no one was there. Releasing the breath she didn't realize she was holding, she returned her attention to the scarecrow. It was looking straight ahead, studying something on the ground.

A huge crow appeared from the corn, circling over the scarecrow and then landing on its arm. Mary wondered if it might be one of the birds who took Cindy. *Definitely big enough.* She started moving forward, scanning the ground for any holes.

A scream pulled her attention from the ground in time to see the scarecrow disappear into the stalks. *What's going on?* As the laughter began again, she picked up her pace until another scream had her running. Her ankle buckled as her foot landed on a dirt clod, forcing her to stumble forward into a clearing.

Mary regained her balance and skidded to a stop. A gasp slipped out as the scarecrow glanced back before returning its attention to Cindy. She knelt before the being, her arms outstretched, tears streaming down her face. The scarecrow raised its arm high, a sickle clutched in its gloved hand.

"NO!" Mary cried as the sickle slashed down, catching Cindy on the side of her neck and slicing through with a spray of blood.

Cindy teetered a moment, her gaze shifting from the scarecrow to Mary, then her head rolled from her shoulders to the dusty ground below as her body fell backward with a gush of blood.

A wordless howl tore from Mary as she stepped toward her friend. The scarecrow bent over, grasped Cindy's head by her hair, and turned to hold it up for Mary to see.

"Such a bountiful harvest," it said in a raspy voice as it lifted Cindy's head above its own, letting her blood drip onto its burlap face.

Bile rose in Mary's throat, and she spewed vomit on the ground. She gave one last look at her friend's body in the dirt before rushing back into the corn. She pushed herself harder as the dry, raspy laughter followed her through the stalks.

CHAPTER TEN

Jane spun and rushed into the cornrows, glancing back one last time at Frank. A sob ripped from her chest as the hooded man slammed his hatchet into the back of Frank's head, splattering the ground with his blood and brains. She forced her attention forward as she stumbled over the uneven ground.

Don't fall or you will end up like Frank. Jane wondered if that would be such a bad thing. Of course, she feared the man wanted more than her blood. She didn't plan on sticking around to find out. Her vision blurred as tears ran freely down her cheeks. She wiped at her face, struggling to keep her sight clear.

The cornrow ran straight through the field, with new rows branching off every five to ten feet. Hopelessness flooded her as the corn seemed never-ending. Jane chanced a glance back; the hooded man walked behind, but she thought she was pulling away.

Her ankle buckled, sending her face-first into the packed dirt. The air rushed from her lungs, and she crawled on the ground, gasping for breath. Squeals of delight came from the hooded man as he made his way closer. Jane rolled on her back, scooting away as her feet pushed against the dirt. Her eyes bulged as the hooded man unclasped the first strap of his overalls and reached for the other.

"Just watchin' ya run gets the juices flowin'," he said with a chuckle. "Nothin' makes me harder than when one of y'all think ya might escape."

Her eyes moved down to the noticeable bulge in his overalls. A whimper slipped past her lips as she slowly began to regain her breath. *Just in time for him...*Jane couldn't finish the thought, her stomach turning to water.

"Don't ya worry none," he said, his voice suddenly husky, "the mask stays on."

As he popped the second clasp, a blur sped from the corn stalks and slammed into the man with a scream of rage. Jane scrambled to her feet as the hooded man's overalls tangled with his legs and forced his balance off enough to knock him to the ground. She watched open-mouthed as Mary kicked the hooded man in his exposed groin. He squealed, this time in pain.

"Move it," Mary hissed, reaching out to grab Jane's hand as she rushed by her.

They ran down the cornrow, pausing long enough to glance back and make sure he wasn't following. The hooded man lay on the ground, holding his crotch and screaming curses their way. Mary offered a nod and pulled Jane with her as she started to run again.

"There's more than one," she said between gulps of air. "We need to get out of this corn."

They sped up as howls of anger followed them through the stalks. Jane glanced back, but the hooded man was still tangled up on the ground. She let out a yelp as Mary suddenly changed direction and pulled her along.

They crashed into the stalks, forcing Jane to slip behind Mary as they pushed through the tighter rows. After a few crossings, they turned back onto a wider row and slowed to a trot. Mary spun in a circle, staring through the corn.

"Maybe we lost him?"

Jane wrapped her arms around Mary and buried her face against her shoulder. Her body shook as she sobbed in relief. Mary held her tight, rubbing her back and offering soothing noises to calm her down.

"Honey, we need to move," Mary said after a few minutes. "No telling just how far away those things really were."

Jane pulled back with a nod. "Thanks...he was going to..." She didn't finish as she began to tremble. After a moment, she blew out a long breath, suddenly realizing they were missing one. "Where's Cindy?"

All Mary could offer was a shake of her head as tears flooded her eyes. She grabbed Jane's hand and started walking. After a few feet, she picked up the pace, and Jane moaned. She couldn't remember the last time she ran this much.

CHAPTER ELEVEN

Mary squeezed Jane's hand tighter, worried she was pulling away. She knew she should slow down, but those monsters were still out there. As she scanned the tops of the cornstalks, she spotted a large rectangle. The setting sun blinded her a bit, keeping all but the outline in shadows.

"Jane," she said as she slowed down and shielded her eyes. "Hey, I think that's a sign...like for a motel or restaurant."

Jane could only nod as she struggled to catch her breath. Mary slipped an arm around her and offered a quick hug. The two hurried forward with Jane continuing to glance back every few steps. They came to the edge of the field and stopped, hiding in the shadows.

The large rectangle read The Donn Motel. It flickered on and off as if someone couldn't decide if it was dark enough. Mary shuddered as she studied two large crows perched upon the sign. They cried out as their heads turned this way and that, giving the appearance they were searching for someone. *Searching for us.*

"Crows attacked Cindy and me," she whispered to Jane, motioning with her head towards the birds.

Jane looked at the sign and then at Mary with wide eyes. "I think we can handle some fucking birds. There's a rapist and murderer searching for us. We need to find a phone...get some help for us, for Cindy."

Mary bit her bottom lip. *There's no help coming that could do anything for Cindy except bury her.* The thought blared in her head, but she only nodded and stepped from the field's edge.

The crows picked up their cries and began to hop around the sign. The women's steps quickened as they rushed towards the motel's lobby.

As they crossed the road, Mary tensed up, expecting the birds to fly at them at any second. They continued to cry out, but they stayed on the sign, watching the women move closer to the motel. Once they stepped onto the parking lot, the crows grew quiet.

"Maybe those are different ones?" Jane offered as they stepped out of the birds' view and moved to the main door.

Mary shrugged, her body tight with fear. *They could still attack, still carry one of us to the scarecrow.* Cindy's severed head flashed in front of her, and she stumbled into Jane, who had come to a stop.

"Welcome weary traveler. Your journey nears its end...it fucking better," Jane said as she read the sign in the window out loud. She moved to open the door but found it locked.

"What? No...is it closed down?"

Mary stepped back and studied the building, hoping for any signs of life.

"Can I help you ladies?" a voice called out.

They spun around, Jane pushing her sister behind her. Sighs of relief slipped out when they saw the patrol car. Mary suspected the driver was studying them as they reflected back in his sunglasses.

"Some...people attacked us," Jane said. "My husband and my sister's friend are in the cornfields."

The officer opened his door, stepped from the vehicle, and stood with his hands on his hips. "So, two are out there with the scarecrow?"

Jane nodded.

"Hold on," he said, stepping around the women to open the door. "Why is it locked? There should be at least a couple more hours before the lockdown."

Mary glanced at Jane before returning her attention to the deputy. *What is he talking about?* She moved to ask Jane, but he spun around and pointed to his vehicle.

"Okay, ladies, I need you to show me exactly where this happened, so hop in."

He held the back door open and waited for the two women to slide in.

The deputy settled into his seat with a sigh. He grabbed the microphone to his radio and held it to his mouth. "Dispatch, this is Deputy Garr. I have..." he glanced back at Jane, and after a moment, she responded.

"Oh...Jane and Mary Lipman."

"Jane and Mary Lipman," he repeated before continuing. "We have a ten-ninety-one. Can you have the Sheriff head out to the Donn Motel?"

The radio squawked, and Deputy Garr put the car in drive and pulled onto the road.

As they drove away, Mary turned to look at the motel. *If he is having the Sheriff come here, why are we leaving?*

Jane pulled Mary close, wrapping her arms around her. Leaning closer, Jane brushed her lips against her sister's ear. "I'm not sure this guy is on the up and up. You see a chance, you run. Find help, but most importantly, get away from here."

Mary glanced at her, eyes wide and shiny with tears. Jane made a shushing noise, warning her sister to stay quiet.

The car picked up speed as they rushed down the road. Deputy Garr stayed quiet, glancing at his mirrors every few moments.

What is he looking for?

CHAPTER TWELVE

Sheriff Smite jumped when the phone rang on his desk. His styrofoam cup tipped over, pouring coffee all over the day's paperwork. He grabbed the cup and swiped as much off the desk as he could before it ruined everything. The damp papers landed in the trashcan to the side.

Thought maintenance wasn't supposed to install the new phones until next week.

The shrill ring continued. Smite reached over just to stop the skull-piercing sound. He held the receiver to his ear. Pops and crackles came over the line before a whispered voice said the sheriff's name.

"Hello?" Smite responded. "Who is this?"

A steady hiss drowned out the answer. Smite pressed the receiver tighter against his ear as he plugged his other ear with his finger. Whispered voices fought to be heard over the hiss, but no matter how hard he concentrated, Smite couldn't make out their words.

"Who the hell is this?" he said, his voice rising with each word.

The whispers grew quiet.

What is going on with this phone? He began to move the receiver away to inspect it when a sudden and intense howl sounded from the earpiece. His head ached from the sudden blast of noise so close to his ear.

"You will stay away," a voice spoke as the howl softened to static. "Or you will join your man in this year's harvest."

The phone went dead as a knock sounded on his door.

"What?" he barked out with a quiver in his voice.

The door swung open, and Janice stepped in. He moved to hang up the receiver.

"Garr called in and requested your presence at the Donn Motel," she said, pausing a moment to see if he had any orders before turning to leave. As she stepped out of the room, she glanced back. "What's with the phone? They aren't scheduled to be working until Tuesday."

Smite let the receiver fall to his desk. *I was just getting used to Garr.*

CHAPTER THIRTEEN

The patrol car came to a stop next to Frank's car. The doors were still open. Garr slipped out and stood by the car for a long moment.

Why isn't he letting us out? Jane hugged her sister, hoping to give her some reassurance.

"What is he doing?" Mary asked, pressing her face against the window.

The deputy stepped to the edge of the corn and cupped his hand around his mouth.

"Can you hear what he's saying?" Jane asked.

Mary shook her head. "But he's coming back."

Jane pulled her sister away from the door and held her tight. Garr moved to the door, pulled it open, and motioned for them to get out.

"Okay, ladies, I need you to walk me through this," he said as he pointed to the abandoned car.

Jane loosed her grip, letting her sister go before slipping out of the car and putting herself between the officer and Mary. She guided her to the middle of the blacktop.

"Someone shot out the tires. The girls went down the road to look for the motel. I stayed with Frank. He was injured. We moved to follow once he woke up, but the crows..." Jane trailed off as a crow landed on the top of the squad car.

"Yeah, they're everywhere," Garr said with irritation. "Go on."

"We ran to the cornfield...there."

Garr turned to see where she pointed before walking back to the edge. He gazed into the rows. The women began to walk backward away from the cars, their eyes locked on the four crows watching them. One hopped to the edge of the roof and let out a cry. Garr spun around.

"Where did these all come from?" he asked as he stepped back towards the road.

A shadow appeared in the cornrows and flashed towards the officer, driving a pitchfork into his back and raising him in the air. Jane and Mary screamed as the scarecrow flung the bleeding man from the prongs to the ground. The crows sprang into the air and descended onto the body. Their angry cries drowned out his pleading screams for mercy.

Jane turned to run, her hand grabbing Mary's to pull her into motion. Laughter chased them as they rushed into the corn.

CHAPTER FOURTEEN

The corn stalks whipped against them as they blindly ran. Jane held up her free hand, hoping to protect her face. Loud cries sounded overhead as the crows flew above them. They ran towards the sinking sun, the light striking Jane in the eyes and stealing her sight.

Mary cried out as she pulled free of Jane's grip. The crows' caws grew in intensity as they circled overhead. Jane slid to a stop, spinning to scramble back. Mary lay on her stomach, her face in the dirt.

"Come on," Jane said as she pulled on her sister's arms.

Mary stayed limp, shaking as soundless sobs wracked her body. The crows' circle tightened, pulling closer to the tops of the corn stalks.

Their cries were coming so quickly, they began to sound like taunting laughter.

Jane glanced up as she continued to tug on her sister.

"Fuck off," she howled to the birds, tears of frustration streaking down her face. "Damn it, Mary, get up."

The stalks began to sway as a stiff wind blew through the cornfield. A path formed between the corn, crossing over the rows already there and allowing her to view straight to the road. The scarecrow stood with the pitchfork in hand. She froze, suddenly struggling to breathe.

The scarecrow reared back and flung the pitchfork down the newly formed path.

Her eyes followed the projectile as it grew closer. *Move!* The thought echoed in her head, but she stayed rooted to the spot. A soft moan slipped out as the blood-covered prongs filled her vision.

The sun slipped lower in the sky, casting shadows like a net over the cornfield. *Dusk in Texas...a good time to die.* The thought sent a shiver down her spine, and she closed her eyes. Jane stumbled back from the force of the blow and tumbled to the ground with a grunt. Surprise filled her at the lack of pain, but there was a weight that, while at first strange, had a sense of familiarity that forced her to open her eyes.

"No," she whispered as she saw Mary laying on top of her, crushing her with her dead weight.

Mary wore a smile on her lips, but her sparkling green eyes were flat and empty as they stared at Jane. The shaft of the pitchfork swayed in the breeze as it stood out from Mary's back. A thin trickle of blood ran from the corner of her mouth, a drop hanging from her chin.

Jane's throat tightened, and her eyes began to blur with tears, but not before she saw the scarecrow was hurrying towards them. A sudden burst of panic pushed Jane to her feet. She gripped Mary by the wrist and began to drag her sister's limp body away from the approaching strawman.

The crows resumed their cries, no longer sounding like laughter but screeches filled with frustration and distress.

The shadows deepened as the sun was all but gone, and Jane wondered what exactly she thought she was doing. The scarecrow was closing ground, and with her sister's added weight, Jane knew there was no escape. Yet she refused to stop moving back, and the thought of letting go of Mary was unimaginable.

Her ears ached from the racket the crows were producing as they flew closer and closer to her head. She hunched down, hoping to provide a smaller target, but it slowed down her backward shuffle even more. The scarecrow slowed to a walk, so close now she could see the stitched-on smile that gave its face a demonic quality. Her breaths came in large huffs as she struggled to pull faster.

"The harvest is at an end, and you two will be pristine additions," the scarecrow said in a raspy whisper.

The last bit of sunlight flittered away, plunging the cornfield into darkness.

Jane stumbled backward as Mary's weight simply disappeared. She landed on her back, driving the air from her lungs and striking her head against a rock jutting up from the hard-packed earth. Stars filled her vision before blurring away to nothingness.

CHAPTER FIFTEEN

Jane woke to bright sunlight filtering in between slits in a set of cheap plastic blinds. Her head ached. She moved to rub at her temple and was startled to discover her arms handcuffed to the bars that ran the length of the bed.

"Hello?" she called out, blinking to clear her vision.

A door opened. A man in a uniform stepped into the room. He studied Jane with a flat expression before closing the door behind him. He stepped over to the far wall, grabbed the chair there, and dragged it a few feet away before sitting down.

Jane started to ask a question but closed her mouth when he held up a finger. He scooted to the end of the chair and leaned forward, his elbows resting on his knees and his hands pressed together in front of his face. Jane found herself growing uncomfortable under the stranger's gaze but kept quiet.

"What do you remember, Mrs. Lipman?"

Fragments of memories flashed through her head: the hooded man, the scarecrow, Frank and Mary's deaths. Tears ran down her cheeks as her throat tightened, cutting off any attempt at speech.

"Ah, well then, we have a problem, you and I," he said softly. "The harvest is over and yet...here you are."

Jane continued to stare at the man, hoping her confusion reflected clearly on her face. "Where is Mary?"

The man leaned back in the chair, crossed his arms, and sighed. "Mrs. Lipman...Jane, you know they are all gone. What you need to focus on right now is what role you'll play from this point forward."

Jane shook her head, a low wail slipping from her lips as a memory replayed ...

She woke up, holding her sister's arm by the wrist, a clean slice right through the forearm, and a pool of blood off to the side. She hugged the arm to her chest.

When she stood, Jane spotted the scarecrow on his perch. She turned and ran, cradling the last bit of her sister tight as she crashed through the corn stalks, the cries of the crows following after her like laughter.

"I found you walking down the center of the road holding a woman's arm and babbling about a scarecrow," the man said with a sigh. "No one is going to believe you. I know what's going on, and I don't believe it. So here are your choices. You can tell your story about monsters killing everyone out there and wind up in the loony bin with your sister's murder pinned to your chest. Won't be the first person put away to stop the truth from being heard."

Jane grunted; her skin crawled at the thought of being locked away in a madhouse. *And yet how will I avoid it?*

"Or, and this one will be hard, those with you will go down as missing persons and you will never speak about what happened. You promise to do that and I'll let you go. Do you understand?"

Jane locked eyes with the man. They were a clear, deep blue, and while she might have described them as gentle or kindly if seeing them under different circumstances, today she saw only cruelty and fear. *Ain't a damned thing you can do in a crazy house.*

She offered the man a nod. Like he said, harvest season is over. There's time enough to figure out all this man knew about the cornfield and its inhabitants. *But first, I need to get out of here.*

The man studied her a moment in silence, then released a sigh. He stood and stepped closer. His hand shot out to grip her jaw tightly. He reached into his back pocket and pulled out a pocket knife, pausing a moment to click it open with his thumb. A look of disappointment bloomed across his face as his fingers slipped into her mouth to grip her tongue.

DONN, TX 1969

"I wish I could believe you, but in the end...better safe than sorry."

-END-

SOMEWHERE IN TEXAS, 1865 ...

CHAPTER ONE

Eli Larkin spat into the dirt. He was happy to be heading home but frustrated that they lost the war. He hadn't left Philadelphia all those years ago to help Texas win her freedom from the greasers just to let those Union bastards show up telling them what to do. Not that he disagreed, but it was the principle of it all.

"Shit," he mumbled as he unstopped his canteen, raising it to his lips to finish off the last bit of water he'd been saving. He couldn't wait to get back to the farm so he could drink something that didn't leave such a tinny aftertaste. That alone would ease the pain of losing to those damn Yankees.

Eli shook his head while he slipped the stopper back. He knew it wouldn't, not deep down where it counted. Oh well, Ruth and the children would forgive him. They were against him going off from the beginning. *Bless her soul; she didn't believe in fighting to keep another in chains no matter what their skin color.*

Another day and he'd be home, or at least where he'd left his family. *Shit, wasn't about to leave my wife and children alone with those bloody redskins roaming about.* The whispered stories of what those savages were up to while the states were fighting each other made his blood run cold; stuff that made the war look like a tea party. In the end, all he could do was hope that was all they were...stories.

He tugged on his bowler, hoping to stop the setting sun from blinding him. Sitting up straight, he pulled the reins to stop his horse. Nervous energy swept from the rider into the beast, and it began to turn around while blowing out huge breaths. Eli patted her neck and offered some soothing words to settle her down. *The corn must be close.*

He thought the preacher had lost his mind when he ordered four groups of three crosses put up on the outskirts of the cornfield, but in the end, the man was proven right. Eli still broke into a cold sweat every time he thought of being forced to put a crazed Abraham down after he ate corn from those cursed stalks.

The image of that young boy's body at his feet, his face beaten past recognition, still haunted him in his dreams. The crosses went up quickly after that, warning people where the cursed land began and ended. Many used them as a way to mark the areas to avoid.

Eli scanned the horizon, nodding when the crosses came into view. He gave a start and then reached into his pack to retrieve his binoculars.

Can't say those Union boys gave me nothin'. He smiled as he remembered coming across them clutched in the hand of a dead Union Officer. He'd always wanted a pair, but before the war, the cost was too excessive. He raised them to his eyes and brought them into focus.

Surrounding the cornfields stood a total of twelve crosses, three on each side, yet this time something was different. He leaned forward as if to convince his eyes what they were seeing was true. Crows sat on the tops of the crosses, hopping up and down to the cross beams before returning to the top. Shapes hung from eleven of the twelve, the empty one serving as a perch for the largest number of the blackbirds.

Each cross easily stood fifteen feet high so they could be seen over the always mature stalks. Eli's thoughts wandered to his bible, tucked snug in his pack. The very bible the preacher had used to bless each cross. He had then told everyone to move far enough away that only the crosses could be seen.

Eli dropped the binoculars back into his pack and stroked the horse's neck. He wasn't close enough to make sense of what he witnessed through the binoculars. When he rode past those crosses over a year ago, they were empty. There was no choice but to investigate, no matter how difficult it was to get the horse closer.

"Come on, girl, it won't be so bad," he said as he patted her once more on the neck.

Eli guided the horse closer to the cornfield. At first, she refused to move more than a few steps before needing more encouragement. He blew out a breath in frustration. *Sun's gonna set before I get close enough to see anythin'.* He dug in his heels, forcing the horse to bolt forward. As they drew nearer, he tensed in anticipation of a struggle, but his mount simply rushed ahead as if embracing her fate.

As they approached, the crows began to caw as they shifted from the crosses until they all perched upon the ones facing Eli. His skin crawled as he realized they were studying him. He pulled up, stopping ten feet away from the crosses. His throat caught when he recognized the preacher nailed to the cross.

Eli slipped from the horse, removing his rifle from the saddle scabbard. He studied the corn as he approached the crosses. The birds' cries intensified with each step, hammering his ears with a wall of noise. A stiff breeze rustled through the cornstalks. He stopped a few feet short and gazed up.

The preacher was bare-chested, wearing only his dark trousers. Thick ropes bound his arms to the cross beams, while thick iron spikes stuck out from his wrists. His legs came together at the feet, where a third spike pinned them to the stipe. Dried blood covered the man's torso, sides, and face as haphazard gashes decorated his skin. Eli shaded his eyes as he took in the damage.

He grew to expect to see such savagery during the war but not so close to his doorstep. *What was the preacher doing outside his church?* Before Eli had left, this very man swore to protect those left behind. A sense of dread crept up his spine, growing heavy in his chest as he moved to the next cross.

The crows quieted, their dark eyes glued to Eli as he stepped past their perch to the next occupied cross. His breath caught when he recognized the bright red hair of the preacher's daughter. Her face, frozen in a twisted expression of pain and horror, seemed more suited for a demon than a child of God.

He found her nudity uncomfortable, remembering how prim and proper the girl behaved before the war. Massive slashes covered her graying skin, and dried blood and slimy mucus covered her from head to toe. *Where are her breasts?* His eyes traveled down, spotting maggots crawling through her bushy pubic mound. Eli's cheeks grew hotter, and he averted his eyes, embarrassed to witness the young woman in such a state. The crows picked up their cries, mocking him with what sounded like laughter to his ears.

His chest tightened as he trotted parallel to the cornfield. There were nine more crosses. The same number of people left under the church's care when Eli went to fight the North.

CHAPTER TWO

The sun dipped below the horizon as darkness blanketed the land. Eli shuddered in relief as he no longer bore witness to his wife's exposed body hanging before him. He rested on his knees, his hands clenching the dry grass as ragged breaths tore from his chest. A red-hot fury filled him until the tears on his cheeks seemed to steam.

Eli spat off to the side. If there was a way, he'd see whoever did this burn in Hell. Grabbing his rifle, he stood and walked back to his horse. She leaned her head down, bumping him on the shoulder. He paused to pat her on the neck, appreciative of the sudden contact. Slipping the saddle from the horse's back, he went through the motions, hoping to forget the horrible vision of his family if but for a moment.

The moon slipped free from behind the clouds, illuminating Eli's surroundings. He focused on the horse, then his camp, then finally chanced a glance at the crosses. The crows were quiet, sleeping in groups upon their perches. The corn stalks swayed as a gentle breeze moved over the field. Eli was grateful it led away, even though the scent of the dead didn't have the same effect on him as before the war.

He slumped to the ground, resting his back against his saddle. His horse wandered a few feet off, searching for some grass to munch on. Eli rested his rifle across his knees as he stared straight ahead, his eyes vacant. *Tomorrow, I'll bury them proper and then hunt down the bastards who did this.* He struggled to keep his eyes open, afraid of what he might see if he allowed them to close. Yet as the hours stretched, he had no choice but to slip into a restless slumber.

CHAPTER THREE

Eli opened his eyes, unsure exactly when he'd closed them. It was still dark; the moon stayed hidden and a heavy fog rolled over the land. He sat up, rifle in hand, listening to the dark.

"Daddy?"

Eli's throat tightened as he struggled to his feet. The voice came from the corn. He was sure of it. *But how?* He stepped towards the field, the fog swirling around him and obscuring everything more than a few inches from his face. Strange noises issued from either side, slithering, scratching, and muted screeching that made his skin crawl. He hesitated as the noises around him gained volume.

"Daddy...I'm scared."

"Hold on, baby girl, I'm comin'," he shouted, tapping into that promise to find the strength to continue.

Dry laughter issued from the darkness, riding on the fog until it, too, was swirling around Eli, chilling him to the bone. Cocking the rifle, he clenched his jaw and pushed forward. The laughter mixed in with the noises from the dark, filling his ears with a steady hiss. Ignoring it the best he could, Eli focused on the thought his daughter was surrounded by the same and hurried to find her.

"Baby girl?" he called out with each step, hoping to pinpoint her location, yet the only answer was the ever-growing hiss.

The moon reappeared, casting its light down to form a misty path in front of him. The fog thickened on each side, muting the hiss. Eli quickened his steps, no longer afraid of running into something out in the dark. At the end of the path stood a young girl surrounded by the intensifying moonlight.

Tears streamed down Eli's face as he raced towards the girl. The mist swirled around her, lifting her dress and hair as if she stood in a stiff breeze. Laughter bubbled from his chest as he scooped her up with one arm, pulling her tight against him. He buried his face into her silky hair, breathing deep the scent of the soap his wife always used. His throat burned with bile as the image of his wife's mutilated face popped into his head, her naked flesh covered in gashes as she hung from the cross.

The scent shifted to death and decay, causing Eli to gag.

He opened his eyes, horrified to find he no longer held his lively little girl but her rotting corpse. Vomit spewed from his mouth, splattering the body before splashing onto the ground. His legs turned to jelly, and he sagged to his knees. His rifle slipped from his hand, landing with a thud, but he clung to his little girl. Eli became lightheaded as the scent of death overwhelmed him once again.

The dry, wispy laughter resumed as the corn began to sway. Eli rocked back and forth, his throat so tight he could only mouth the words to his children's favorite lullaby. The field plunged into darkness a moment, and then the moonlight returned, shining down a few feet before him. In the illumination stood a man dressed all in white.

Eli stared, his mouth agape, as the man stepped towards him. He was unlike anyone Eli had ever seen before. The man stood seven feet tall and had limbs slightly longer than one would expect, even at that height. His long black hair was slicked back and hung to his shoulders, and his skin was so pale, Eli wondered if even the moonlight might burn him.

The Pale Man offered a smile with blood-red lips, exposing razor-sharp teeth that seemed to overfill his mouth. A thin tongue snaked out and ran over his bottom lip before slipping back inside. He knelt on one knee before Eli and reached out to stroke the corpse's hair.

"Does not seem fair," he said in a voice much higher pitched than Eli expected. It held a musical quality that plucked at the sorrow in his heart.

Eli stared at The Pale Man, struggling to understand his meaning but agreeing with his words completely. He finally offered a nod.

The Pale Man smiled once again, this time his lips just barely twitching upward before returning to a straight line.

"He promised you and yours eternal life," The Pale Man said as he pointed to the body of the preacher. "I am going to let you in on a secret...there is no salvation for those killed on these grounds. As if they did not suffer enough in their final moments, their fate is now damnation and hellfire."

Eli locked gazes with The Pale Man, unable to turn away. The angry heat from earlier filled his belly as rage began to flow through him.

The Pale Man stood, stepped back a few feet, and motioned to the crosses. "Now, while his promises might have fallen short, mine will not. I can offer your family the peace they so richly deserve."

After a moment of silence, Eli croaked out, "How?"

"By giving you what you so desperately want...retribution," the man said, spinning in a circle with his arms outstretched.

Eli glanced down at his daughter. He would give anything to make them pay. He let her body slip from his grasp before crawling forward.

The man stepped forward, grasped Eli by the arms, and lifted him to his feet. He leaned closer, his lips brushing against Eli's ear. "You will become my harvester here on Earth, and for that, I will gift you a soul for a soul. I will give you all that you need to recognize those responsible. It will be up to you to make them pay for their affront on these children of God."

"That it?" Eli asked.

"Is that not enough?"

Eli thought a moment, then nodded. As long as they suffer, it will be.

CHAPTER FOUR

Eli woke with a start. A foggy haze hung low over the ground. He wiped at his face, unsure if the moisture was from the morning dew or his own tears. *It musta been a dream...no matter how real she felt in my arms.*

The sun began its slow crawl into the sky, burning off the last bit of fog and bathing the corn in a soft yellow glow.

Eli struggled to his feet, pressing his palm to his forehead. His stomach rumbled with a hollowness he understood couldn't be filled with food. A loud single caw pulled his attention to the crosses. He stumbled toward the corn, struggling to comprehend what he saw. Each cross now stood empty save for a single crow.

Eli rushed to the cross his wife had hung from just hours ago. He turned in a circle as if the bodies may suddenly appear. Falling to his knees, he stared at the ground, unsure what to do. A breeze moved through the corn, bringing wispy laughter to his ears. His head jerked up, rage burning hot in his belly.

Three crows now sat, perched on the cross before him. Each appeared to be studying him with its dark eyes. After a moment, the middle crow hopped down to the ground and issued a cry. Eli's eyes followed the bird's gaze to the ax leaning against the stipe. He crawled forward until he was close enough to reach out and grasp the ax handle.

"The preacher was wrong," he said to the crow as it studied him from the side. "This place shouldn't be contained. It needs to be free, free to cleanse the world."

Eli stood, drawing back the ax and slamming it down into the stipe. As the wood chips flew from each blow, Eli channeled his rage into the steady swing of the ax. *If I hurry, I might finish before nightfall.*

CHAPTER FIVE

Eli's arms ached as the eleventh cross fell to the ground. He tied it to his saddle and urged the horse to pull it to the other ten off to the side of the field.

"One more and then rest," he said as he unhooked the cross.

Eli patted her neck, leaving a bloody handprint, before moving back to the cornfield. He hefted the ax as he stepped up to the final cross. His blood made the handle slick, and he wondered if he had enough strength left to finish the job as the sun slipped down. A loud cry pulled his attention up, and he studied the crows sitting upon the crossbar.

The largest hopped into the air, flying over the cornfield and then slipping into the stalks and out of sight. The next one followed and so on until all the birds were now somewhere in the corn. Their cries grew in volume, and Eli thought his ears would burst from the noise. He let the ax slip from his fingers as he entered the corn. The birds grew quiet as he approached.

They stood in a circle; the largest in the middle. Eli stared at the ground, unsure what to do. The crow pecked at the soil before taking to the air, and the others once again followed the leader, taking off with loud cries. The last rays of sunlight cut through the cornfield, blinding him.

The laughter returned, riding the breeze as Eli's vision slowly cleared. He raked his fingers across the dirt, pushing piles of the hard, dry earth to the side. Moonlight filtered through the clouds, shining through the stalks as if to guide his hands. His body ached from the long day of work, but a frenzy overcame him as he dug deeper into the soil.

Eli paused when his fingers scraped against rough material, then he pulled it up. He held a cloth bag, tied at the neck with a thin braid of dark string. *Is that hair?* He was all but sure it was as he gripped the end and pulled. The sack slumped open, releasing a pocket of air like a wheeze. He took a deep breath, ignoring the dread washing over him as he turned it over to let the contents tumble to the ground.

Three items fell to the dirt: a rusty old scythe with a wooden handle, a pair of black gloves, and a balled-up piece of burlap. The wind died down, and a hush settled over the field. He couldn't explain it, but Eli knew these were the instruments of his revenge. He picked up the burlap, holding it flat so he could get a better look in the moonlight.

Dark round stones appeared stitched to the rough brown material, but Eli couldn't make out how. More stitching was used to make an outline of a smile that gave the mask a surprisingly sinister look. As he stared at the mask, building up the courage to take the next step, the breeze carried a voice to his ears.

"Once you don the mask, you will be able to follow the trail of the men responsible. You will have only three days, as we are at the end of the harvest, but fear not...I have gifted you with all you need to make them pay. For your exchange to take place, there is but one rule. Those responsible must die on these lands. Failure to do so will lead to your loved ones reliving the atrocities done to them at the end of their lives for an eternity."

Eli shuddered. He could only imagine what each one suffered before their final breaths.

"It is the least you can do since you failed so spectacularly to save them," the voice whispered before resuming the wispy laughter from Eli's dreams.

His throat tightened as he brought the mask up. *The least I can do.* He pulled the mask over his face, blocking out the moonlight and, more importantly, the laughter on the wind.

For a moment, there was only darkness, then lightning streaked toward the ground. Earth-shattering explosions deafened Eli until he heard only a low, steady hum. Then the pain began. It was subtle at first, more an itch than anything else. Soon, though, it spread through his body, twisting and tearing through his flesh. His mouth flopped open in a wordless howl of agony, and the lightning continued to strike all around him.

Eli flopped on the ground as if he were a fish pulled from the lake. His mind went blank from the overwhelming pain as his vision took on a red hue. The lightning lessened until plunging him back into darkness. A sob ripped from his chest, the mournful cry taking the place of the hum.

A streak of light slashed across the darkness, hurtling towards the ground at an angle. Eli assumed the light was many different colors, but he witnessed only red. His eyes followed its fall until it struck the ground with an impact that drove it deep into the Earth.

A hush fell over the area, and Eli struggled to sit up. A single bolt of lightning struck from the darkness, impaling him to the ground. His body convulsed with the energy as it flowed through him into the earth below him. His mouth opened once again, but nothing came out save a thick ray of light that burned brighter and brighter until Eli consisted of nothing but pain.

CHAPTER SIX

Eli opened his eyes to find the largest crow studying him. It stood a few feet away, its head twisting back and forth.

You have received a gift. This is your chance to prove yourself worthy.

Even though the words were in his head, he understood they were not his thoughts. He stared at the crow, waiting for it to continue.

We will find those responsible, but you must drive them to the corn, for only in the corn will their deaths have significance.

Eli struggled to his knees. His vision was still tinted red, and he wondered if it was day or night. *Does it matter?* Not only was everything clearer, but his sight seemed to go on much further than ever before. He glanced around, searching for the items he discovered with the mask. The crow hopped back, revealing the gloves and the scythe.

You will need these to carry out your revenge, but know their use comes with a heavy price.

Eli nodded at the bird before crawling over and lifting the gloves. He gave a start as his vision fell upon his hand. At first, he thought something was wrong, but he soon realized he was seeing past the skin and into his flesh. He stared in amazement as his blood flowed through his veins and back towards his heart. Shifting his concentration, he soon found himself staring at his skin, but there was a heat there, a heat that seemed to glow.

Look for my brothers and sisters in the sky, for we will show you the path.

With that final statement, it issued a loud caw that sent all the crows into the sky. Eli watched them fly away as he stood. How was he expected to keep up with the birds? His gaze fell upon his horse, standing a few yards from the edge of the corn. Her head was down as if terrified to even look at him. Slipping the scythe into his belt loop, he stepped closer, his hand out as if he could calm her with his approach.

Tiny sounds of panic issued from the mare, but she stayed in place. As Eli moved closer, the noises ceased but her body began to tremble from the effort. Her front legs gave out, and she tumbled to the ground. Steam rose from her body, and Eli could see her heart slow and finally stop. For a moment, he stood in confusion, but then he hurried to the horse and laid his hands upon her chest.

He stared at the horse's heart, allowing his new vision to show him the organ. *Do I pray?* He dismissed the thought, instead following his instincts to say, "Rise."

Eli's breath caught as the heart began to shudder and pulsate. It expanded in the beast's chest until it filled the entire cavity. Smoke slipped from the mare's nostrils, and after a moment, she opened her eyes. Flames danced within those orbs as she shook her head. Her skin began to smolder, sending wisps of smoke into the air. He stepped closer, holding his hand out to give her a reassuring pat.

The heat rolling off the horse forced him to pull his hand away. Touching her would be impossible, but he was sure he was meant to ride her. He looked at the gloves and after hesitating a moment, decided to slip them on.

The leather was velvety, in fact, the softest thing he'd ever felt next to the first time he held his baby girl. His hands slithered into the gloves, first his left, then the right, and for a moment, he swore they grew tighter around his flesh. He studied the dark leather through his red haze, surprised he no longer could look through the layers as he had a few minutes before.

Eli reached out, the heat no longer an issue, and patted the horse on the neck. He swung up onto the saddle he had no memory of placing on her and gripped the reins.

"Time is short," he said, his raspy voice one he no longer recognized.

He glanced one final time at the single cross. He would take matters into his own hands and seek retribution for those abandoned, consequences be damned. His mount sprang forward as he dug his heels into her flank. Smoke poured from her nostrils as flames leaked from her mouth.

CHAPTER SEVEN

Eli stood next to his mount on a hilltop a mile or so away from a stand of trees his crows floated lazily above in a circle. The trees were fairly young, but all stood at least ten feet high. There was a tugging sensation consistently trying to pull him back the way he had come. Although not quite painful, he understood the longer he stayed away from the cornfield the worse it would become.

The crows sank lower, disappearing into the treetops. With the world washed in red, Eli wasn't quite sure what time of day it was, but he knew time was running out. He swung up onto the mare's back and drove his heels into her flank. The two rushed towards the trees, and he fought the urge to issue a cry, unsure if it was one of wrath or relief.

Sparks flew whenever his mount's hooves struck the ground. More flames slipped from the beast's mouth as their speed increased. Once they neared the edge of the trees, the beginning of an owl's cry was cut short. A man stumbled from the grove, his arms held up high to protect his face and head.

Three crows darted around the man, striking with claws and beaks until the man tumbled to the ground shrieking in agony. Eli slipped from his mount, rushing to the man to drive the crows away. They issued cries of irritation as they circled overhead. He glanced at the man and saw his face and arms were covered with deep slashes. Eli swayed a bit, the scent of the man's blood made him lightheaded.

The knot in his belly untied, releasing hot rage to fill his body until he shook. Slipping the scythe from his belt loop, Eli gripped the man by his hair and pulled him to his knees. Fear radiated from the man's eyes as he pleaded for mercy. Eli's vision darkened, coloring everything in a bloody red.

"There will be no mercy for you," he whispered, his voice like autumn leaves crunching underfoot.

The crows began to caw loudly over each other, causing a wave of noise to wash over the two. The man went limp, staying upright only by the strength of Eli's grip. Raising the scythe, Eli brought it down in a sweeping arch into the man's neck. Blood sprayed out when the blade sliced through the flesh. The man's body tumbled to the ground as Eli lifted the head and stared into its eyes.

The crows descended onto the body, pecking into the exposed flesh and laying in the blood as it pumped from the stump. Eli lifted the head higher, letting the blood drip onto his face mask and soak through, wetting his lips. Heat traveled through his body, following the path of the blood as it slid down to his belly. His rage intensified with each drop until his entire body trembled in fury.

Let the reckoning commence.

The fire was larger than Flynn wanted, but they were deep enough in the grove, he expected no one could see it. He sat with his back against the thickest tree circling the clearing they discovered when searching for a camp. Once the boys cleared it out, there was plenty of room for all of them. *As long as at least two are on guard duty.*

Flynn knew now was the time to catch forty winks, as his most trustworthy men were keeping an eye on both ends. Bones, Johnny Cakes, and Pojo were playing cards near the fire. He pulled his hat down to shade his eyes before crossing his arms. *Been a coon's age since I got any real sleep...*Memories of their recent deeds filled his head, and a smile slipped onto his lips. Just the memory of that woman struggling beneath him gave Flynn a jolt of excitement.

Go to sleep, he shouted in his head. He'd have plenty of time later to relive all the fun he'd had riding that filly. Once people started talking about the warning he'd left, he'd have free reign to take back what was rightfully his. His breathing deepened as he let sleep overtake his thoughts.

Flynn sat up at the abrupt ending to the owl's call. He glanced at the other three, who were still playing cards. He hissed a warning to grab their attention and pointed to the direction the cry came from. "You dumb sons-a-bitches, that was a warning."

"What was?" Johnny Cakes mumbled as Bones gathered the cards. Pojo raked the coins from the pot into his hands and slipped them into his pockets.

"Lord help me," Flynn mumbled as he stood, his Colt in his hand. "Get ready."

The sudden cries of crows filled the grove, drowning out all other sounds. The three men by the fire stepped back, moving towards the shadows. Flynn glanced over his shoulder, noting Mississippi Slim enter the clearing. *Whatever's goin' on wasn't on his side.* He turned his attention in the direction of their other lookout, Jackson.

Flynn shook his head. Jackson was thick as molasses but could handle himself in a scrap. *Anyone dumb enough to come through him will at the least be hurtin' ... unless he's been drinkin' again.* The crows grew quiet, leaving only the sounds of the men's anxious breaths and nervous snorts from their mounts. Flynn slid farther into the shadows, away from the others and closer to the horses.

A dark shadow flew through the trees, entered the clearing, and twirled in a tight circle above the campfire. The flames flared toward the sky as the shadow spun higher and higher. Smaller shadows darted through the clearing, which after a moment, Flynn identified as crows. *Largest crows I've ever seen.*

The crows darted down, lashing out at his men with beaks and talons. The birds' cries mixed with the screams of pain the men issued as they attempted to defend themselves. Random gunshots sounded as they fired blindly.

Fools. Flynn kept his eyes on the side Jackson was covering. Whatever was happening, Flynn would bet his right nut it wasn't just some fucking crows.

The fire was now as tall as a man, and soon Flynn figured those flames would be dancing in the trees. He took a deep breath and gave a quick whistle to his men before rushing towards the horse line. As he reached the skittish equine, Flynn reached up and patted his stallion on the neck.

"What in tarnation?" Mississippi Slim barked out as he slid to a stop next to his mount, gesturing towards all the chaos.

The others soon appeared and climbed on their horses. Flynn reached over to Jackson's mount and pulled him free. *Jackson is either dead or he can walk.* This old stallion had been through hell more than once, and he would be damned if he left him to whatever was going on. The trees began to crackle and split from the heat as the fire moved throughout the branches.

"Boys, time to ride," Flynn shouted as his mount sprang forward into a gallop.

Flynn glanced back as they moved farther away from the grove. Cold fear slithered into his belly when he saw a man calmly step from the blaze. With crows circling around him, the man lifted Jackson's head to let it dangle by the hair.

CHAPTER EIGHT

Eli rode behind the men as the crows herded them back to the corn. At first, they tried to turn away, but each time the crows dove into the men, forcing them back. The men rode on until desperation gave one of them the courage to try again, this time ignoring the crows and pushing his mount to travel west.

Whatever hope he may have handed the others was squelched as his screams of terror filled the air. The crows tore at his body, stripping away his hair and any exposed flesh they could get to before pulling him from his mount. The birds' caws of celebration drowned out the man's cries as they descended on him when he tumbled to a stop.

The others slowed a moment, watching the birds tear their friend apart bit by bit. The largest one turned his head, vomit spraying onto the ground before he drove his heels into his mount and rushed away. The others followed his lead, hopeful the distraction would delay the birds long enough for them to make their escape, Eli guessed. *They will not elude my retribution.*

At first, he was content to let the crows guide the men to their doom, but it was time to make his presence felt. As he pushed his mount, the flames leaking from her mouth grew hotter. Smoke poured from her nostrils and steam rose from her eyes. Her cries took on the sound of a locomotive as it barreled down the track. They would be at the corn soon.

Eli pulled closer to those he hunted, anticipation battling with the ever-present rage that fueled his every move. Time was running out. *Will there be enough time to make them suffer?* He was well aware that once they died in the corn, their suffering would be eternal, but deep down he knew it wouldn't be enough for him. *They need to suffer by my hand.*

With a wave of his hand, the crows took to the air and darted ahead of him, driving the riders closer together. His horse's skin grew hotter as larger flames billowed from the beast. He sensed the corn before seeing the tall stalks swaying in the wind. A weight lifted from his chest at the sight.

The men drove their mounts into the stalks, unable to ride around the field as the crows increased their attacks. The beast beneath Eli let loose a terrible cry of agony before the fires burned through her coat. He leapt from the beast as she tumbled to the ground, turning to ash. Eli landed on his feet and charged into the corn, rushing towards the call of the crows ... his crows.

Flynn wondered where their handiwork was as they rode towards the cornfield. There was only one of those crazy crosses left standing, and someone had removed all the bodies. He didn't go to all that trouble to have his hard work removed. He glanced back, startled to see a horse breathing fire gaining on his men.

Is that the man from the flames?

The fear laying heavy in his belly began to squirm once again. It was time for drastic measures if he hoped to escape, reputation be damned. The stalks swayed as a heavy breeze blew through the field. Flynn guessed there were only a few more hours left until dawn and the end of any chance of escaping this man following them.

"Slim," he hollered over the howl of the wind and the death cries of Pojo. "Once we hit the corn, pull everyone together. If this bastard wants a fight, he's found one."

Flynn leaned closer to his mount's neck as he urged him to pick up speed. The horse responded with a shake of his head and a snort but no acceleration. If Flynn's plan was to work, he needed to be in the corn ahead of the others. Taking a deep breath, he slipped his knife from his belt. *Hate to do this buddy—*

A shriek from behind cut into his thoughts and drowned out all other sound. The cold fear in his belly turned to ice as it slithered throughout his body. His mount sprang forward as fear forced him to find his final reserves. They crashed into the corn, and Flynn glanced back one last time to witness the horse rolling across the ground until it burned away.

This just might work.

CHAPTER NINE

Eli's rage burned red hot. Would he end up like his horse? *Does it really matter?* Eli knew the answer, of course; it only mattered if the men stopped him from freeing his family. Two had died by the birds he now controlled, and while they had suffered, it was a wasted effort. Yet there were still four in the corn, exactly what he needed to hopefully release his family to heaven.

He couldn't be sure, but he thought he had a few more hours left before the end. *Still enough time to make them suffer first.* The crows began to fly the perimeter of the field, making sure no one slipped free and away from their fate. Eli pulled his scythe free and stepped into the stalks.

Now that he was back in the corn, Eli became lighter—in spirit and step. The crows began to cry out, not in warning but what seemed to Eli as singing. He would match their song with the screams of those men and make music no one on Earth would recognize.

Focusing, Eli swept his gaze through the corn as the stalks simply disappeared from his hazy red vision. Three of the men stood by their horses near the center of the field. The fourth, their leader, if Eli guessed correctly, sat atop his horse at the far right corner. A few more feet and the crows' cries would become a warning. *The crows won't let him escape.*

Eli stepped forward. Now was not the time for subtly as Eli's rage coursed through his veins. It built with each step until he shook from the energy. He stopped a few feet from the men, still hidden by corn and the night sky. Although the moon was shining, his world remained blanketed in the same red haze.

The men stood shoulder to shoulder, with the one on the far left holding the reins to the horses in one hand and a Colt in the other. The man in the middle held his rifle to his shoulder, and the one on the far right drew a revolver from each hip. Satisfaction filled Eli as the men trembled, waiting for him to appear.

His body hummed from the anger he held within his form as Eli stepped into the open. He opened his mouth and roared, unleashing the pent-up energy and sending a wave of fear to wash over the men. The horses bolted, pulling the man holding the reins off his feet. They dragged him a few feet before one lashed out with its hind leg, driving its hoof into his forehead with a sickening crunch. He let loose, sliding to a stop. The other men opened fire, crying out in excitement as their bullets tore into Eli's body.

The red haze grew lighter as Eli tumbled backward and fell to the ground. Intense pain radiated through the injuries, pulsating as if in rhythm to his heartbeat. The slugs pushed through his flesh, pressing against his skin for a moment before tearing through. The pain ceased and his vision darkened.

The crunch of footsteps moved closer. He laid still, his fingers tightening around the scythe's handle. At the sound of the man pulling back the hammer, Eli lashed out. The scythe sliced through the man's left leg at the calf. Blood squirted onto Eli as the man crashed to the ground. He fired off three random shots into the sky while howling in pain. Eli sat up, reached over to the man's stump, and began to dig into the exposed meat.

His fingers gripped the bone and jerked down, tearing it free from the man's knee. The man's howls turned into shrieks, and his eyes rolled back into his head. Eli drove the shard of bone into his chest, pinning him to the ground.

A hush fell upon the corn. Eli stood and pointed to the last man standing.

"How are you still alive?" the man cried out as his rifle slipped from his hands.

"It is through my Master's will," Eli replied in a raspy whisper.

Dark arms broke through the ground around the corpse. They dug into the flesh, splattering the ground with more blood. The last man's gaze locked on his friend's body, ignoring Eli as he drew closer. He fell to his knees, arms outstretched, screaming to the sky for mercy.

"Mercy?" Eli's hot rage burned as he repeated the word, "Mercy?"

He slashed down, swiping the scythe through the man's face at an angle. Blood bubbles gurgled at the man's lips as time seemed to slow. Eli waited until the top part of the man's head slid off, exposing his brains, nasal cavity, and lower half of his jaw. The remaining eye blinked one last time before Eli kicked out, driving the man to the ground.

The night sky began to lighten as dawn approached. An unseen force began to pull at Eli, attempting to drag him to the cross left standing. He shook his head, leaning toward the direction of the last man. The leader.

"I was promised retribution," he whispered as he ground his boots into the soil and pushed forward, "and retribution, I will have."

Flynn spun his mount, panic overwhelming his senses. The horse bolted towards the edge of the corn, cries for mercy following him. As he passed the edge of the field, crows darted after him, tearing at his clothes and skin with their talons. The largest crow landed on the horse's head and drove its beak into the equine's right eye.

His horse screamed in pain and tumbled to the ground, pinning his rider beneath his weight. Flynn's head bounced on the ground, stunning him into silence, and his leg snapped under his mount. Waves of pain rolled over him as his mind attempted to process what was going on. The crows landed on the mount, each one staring down at Flynn.

Flynn stared at the horizon as the first rays of the morning appeared. The sky lightened, and he smiled. A loud caw drew his attention away from the sunrise and toward the corn. There stood the man. *Is it a man or some type of monster?* The question sat heavy in his mind as he studied the approaching shape.

Dressed in all black, the man seemed to glide across the terrain. Flynn squinted as the morning light fell upon the man's head. His skin appeared to be burlap, pulled tight over his skull. Where his eyes should be, two black stones stared back at Flynn. They glittered in the sunlight and sent a chill through Flynn's body. There was no warmth radiating from those black orbs, only rage.

Two thick weaves of slightly darker color curled up in a mock smile beneath where a nose should reside. Blood dripped from the scythe in his hand. The crows began to caw, their cries growing in volume the closer the man moved. The sun rose higher, bathing the earth in its warmth, but Flynn knew only the icy fear in his belly.

"Well go on," he said through gritted teeth. The last thing he planned to do was give any satisfaction to this thing.

"See you in Hell," the scarecrow said as he slashed the scythe through Flynn's neck.

CHAPTER TEN

Eli spun to the sound of slow clapping coming from the edge of the cornfield. The Pale Man from his dream stood there with Eli's wife and children. His eyes swept over his family, each one shimmering within his red haze. He stepped forward, but the man held up a hand.

"You may look but not touch," he said with a sly smile.

Eli slammed into an invisible barrier only a few feet from his wife. The anger began to build once again in his belly, filling him with a white-hot rage. "We had a deal."

The Pale Man nodded, the smile broadening upon his lips. "Yes, a soul for a soul. You made no such deal for a touch. Besides, they will not recognize you in such a state."

Eli grew still. There was fear in his wife's eyes and painted on his children's faces. The Pale Man was correct, and it only added fuel to his indignation. A bright light consumed his wife, burning Eli's vision to darkness. When it returned, she was gone. The Pale Man held up one finger. The light returned twice more, each time leaving with another person until only The Pale Man and Eli's baby girl remained.

Laughter bubbled from The Pale Man, and he held up three fingers. "So close, but you fell short."

Eli gestured toward the man under the horse. "Here is your fourth."

The Pale Man's laughter grew in volume as he rested his hand on the little girl's head. "There is nothing I can do with that. He died outside the corn's influence."

Eli trembled as his rage trickled away. He slipped to his knees, knowing he failed but not understanding. He realized the other men died so far away, but this one was so close. *How can a few feet stand in the way?*

"And yet there is still hope, Mister Eli Larkin," The Pale Man said as he lifted baby girl by her head.

Eli reached out, unable to move close enough to do much more than will The Pale Man to stop. "Anything ... just please ... stop."

"To stop this dear child from being ravished in the fires of Hell, I require only for you to become that which I named you earlier, my harvester of souls."

Eli stared at his daughter a moment, trying to memorize everything about her before offering The Pale Man a hesitant nod. There was no decision to make, no price too high to save his daughter from anymore torment. Her form wavered and disappeared in a flash of light. The Pale Man clapped his hands together and offered Eli a slight bow.

The barrier disappeared, and Eli stared blankly ahead.

The crows began to cry once more.

"The season is over," The Pale Man said as he touched Eli's forehead with his right index finger. "For now, you will rest; and when next you rise, you will know what to do."

The crows swooped down and gripped Eli by the shoulders and arms until they had the strength to lift him from the ground. They flew to the final cross and carried him to the top. His feet rested on the sedile of the cross while his arms draped over the cross bar. Eli relaxed as he watched The Pale Man stroll back into the cornfield. The red haze slowly faded as the scarecrow slipped into darkness. The image of a little girl floated in the void for a moment before disappearing with a flicker.

Who was that? His thought boomed in the darkness. *Who am I?*

For a moment, there was only silence, then a whispered answer sounded from the void.

"You are The Scarecrow, my harvester of souls."

SOMEWHERE IN TEXAS, 1926 ...

PROLOGUE

Deputy Raymond Smite stared at the new wooden sign, which the sheriff had driven into the ground last week because all the original signs rotted away ages ago. *Don't really need a sign … no one is dumb enough to come out here.* He glanced at the cornfield just ahead on the other side of the road. *Course, there was a time no one would have laid a road so close to the corn either.*

His eyes settled on the 115hrouge towering over the stalks. A chill rolled through his body, a welcome break from the heat if not for the cause being so close. It was a quarter of a mile away, but Smite knew it could be on top of him before he thought about getting back in the cruiser.

"Damn it, Ray," he mumbled, just to fill the silence. "Harvest is over a month away, so stop being a fraidy-cat."

A crow landed on the top of the blank sign and let out a caw. Startled, Smite jumped and dropped the bucket of paint he was carrying. He scrambled to set it upright so not to spill any while the crow continued to issue its cries. Glaring at the bird, he dusted off the knees of his pants.

"What do you want?" he asked the bird as he began to paint the wood with bright white paint. "I don't have time for your nonsense, so get."

The crow grew quiet, leaning closer and turning its head to study the deputy with its shiny dark eye. Smite's cheeks blazed red, more from the bird's scrutiny than the Texas heat.

"You know why y'all need new signs?" he asked the crow, desperate to fill the silence. "Some fool is gonna build a motel out here. You believe that? A goddamn motel."

The bird issued a cry as it sprang into the air and circled overhead. Smite attempted to ignore the bird, but soon, a shadow fell over him. *Please don't be The Scarecrow.* The thought sent his heart pounding against his chest. He glanced up from his work, and a sigh ripped past his lips. A number of crows now flew overhead in a tight group.

Shade is always welcome. He returned his attention back to the sign and frowned. *Is this enough?* "Welcome to Donn, Texas," he read aloud to the crows overhead. *Is there anything else to include?* He stared at the sign, knowing the answer but aware it wouldn't matter. If he was a kind man, he'd add the warning all the locals already knew.

Smite glanced at the corn and whispered, "Run. Run as far as you can, for when The Scarecrow wakes, the harvest of blood begins."

CHAPTER ONE

Orville Perkins stood at the edge of a small grove of pecan trees on the top of the hill. His jaw tightened as another truck arrived with materials. *Who'd be fool enough to build so close to the corn?* Couldn't be anyone from the area, that was for sure, everyone knew to avoid the corn this time of year.

Sighing, Orville stepped back into the grove. Time was running out, and it didn't seem like those fools were leaving anytime soon. *Gonna have to chance it tonight.* Any longer and there was no telling what might happen. Last thing he wanted was the attention of The Scarecrow. His stomach squirmed just at the thought.

For a moment, he was a young boy again, staring up into those shiny black eyes. He could almost smell the urine he remembered running down his leg as The Scarecrow hopped from its perch and towered over him. The crows had screamed in anticipation as they flew about the corn. Orville had stayed frozen, unable to do anything but stare into those black stone eyes.

"My child," The Scarecrow said with a voice as cold as the grave. "Today is a special day, and I see you've brought me a gift."

The Scarecrow pointed to the ground before Orville as its weird burlap lips curled up in a smile. Orville nodded slowly, unsure what the thing was talking about. He hadn't come bearing gifts. He glanced down at the dead cat at his feet.

"This was just the mangy old tomcat that hangs around my father's barn."

"Every life is precious," The Scarecrow said as it scooped the corpse up with one hand. "For you to bring this creature to me and offer me its essence ... well, my child, that makes my heart swell."

A large crow landed on its extended forearm and leaned over to snatch the cat in its massive black beak. The others began to cry again, filling the air with their song as they landed in a group. The crow hopped down to the dirt, flinging the body to its brothers and sisters. The Scarecrow knelt down, reaching out to pat Orville on his head.

"My flock thanks you for this treat, but that creature is missing the one thing I need more than anything during the harvest season. Do you know what that is?"

Orville didn't, but he nodded.

The Scarecrow slipped a finger under the boy's chin and lifted his head until they made eye contact. "Human souls ... which come from people."

Orville scrunched up his face a moment, struggling to remember something the preacher said the Sunday before, but the memory refused to come.

"Can you bring me a person?" The Scarecrow asked as its head tilted to the side. "They can be good or bad. In the end, it doesn't matter. All that matters is the number collected."

Orville nodded that he understood. His father was just complaining about how little the garden was producing as the family was growing in size. Orville's face lit up as his father's words echoed in his head; too many mouths to feed.

"I can bring you someone," he whispered.

"Then it's a deal," The Scarecrow said as it spun around with its arms raised out. "Bring me a soul every year, and I will make you something special ..."

That was thirteen years ago.

Orville shook his head at the thought. He did what The Scarecrow asked; every year he delivered on his promise, but he made sure never to face it again. He staked the gift before its perch so when it woke, the first one was ready. *But these fool people gonna make me late.*

His bowels turned to water at the thought of facing The Scarecrow again. Orville expected there were a few more hours until sunset. He stepped to the middle of an opening in the grove and studied the woman at his feet. She was pretty, with long dark hair and the greenest eyes he'd ever seen. She wore a tattered sundress he'd found on a clothesline a few days after he took her.

"Well, darlin'," he announced as he moved to unhook his overalls, "I have good news ... looks like we still got some time together."

CHAPTER TWO

Sheriff Pike pulled to a stop in the motel's parking lot. There had been nothing but empty space three weeks ago, but now a U-shaped building sat opposite of the corn. He glanced to the side, realizing the crosses were gone. *This won't do.* His jaw clenched at the thought.

As Pike opened his door, a man appeared from the back end of the motel. He offered a wave as he hurried to the sheriff's vehicle.

"Howdy, Sheriff," Robert Tanner, the owner of the motel, called out. "What brings you out this way?"

"You removed the crosses?"

Confusion flashed over Robert's face before he nodded. "Oh, yeah. The wife found them unsettling. I mean who has that many crosses around their establishment?"

"It's not that simple, Mr. Tanner," he said as he gazed over to the corn. "There was a reason they were there."

"Well, I didn't destroy them, if that's your worry," Robert said, offering a smile.

"Just … put them back up, same way you found would be best," Pike said as he swung his attention back to the motel. "I'll check with the preacher to see if he's gonna need to bless them once again."

"Well … okay," Robert said. "I'll see what I can do. Anything else you need?"

"Just wanted to give you one last warning," Pike said, locking eyes with the man. "You don't want to be here come tomorrow. I don't know why anyone would be fool enough to build anything this close to the corn, but since you did … delay the opening a month. Trust me."

"Are you kidding?" Robert asked with a chuckle. "I didn't just work these men half to death to delay our Grand Opening. Unless you can give me a reason better than just because."

Sheriff Pike stared at the man a moment before shaking his head. "If you can't take my word, well … you'll see soon enough. Just don't forget I warned you."

He gave one last look at the corn before tipping his hat and moving back to his car. Tanner offered a wave and moved back to the building. Pike threw the car into reverse, backed out, and pulled back onto the main road. *Should I have told Tanner the truth? Better yet, would he believe it?* He knew the answer because ten years ago he'd learned the truth ... and he still didn't believe it.

CHAPTER THREE

"Is he gone?"

Robert glanced over to the open door where his wife Ruth stood. He smiled as he nodded. She stepped from the motel and hurried to his side, slipping her arms around him. Trembling, she released a nervous titter as she hugged him tight. He wrapped his left arm around her, and they stood quietly for a moment.

"He was upset about the crosses, huh?" she asked, finally breaking the silence.

"Yep. He may send the preacher, so we best get them back up. I'll have the crew help me before he shows up. That way there's no interference."

"That's good," she said, resting her hand on his arm. "It will all be worth it … you'll see."

Robert nodded, suddenly unable to speak as his throat tightened. They were coming up on the first anniversary. *I'd move heaven and earth to see her again.*

Ruth stepped back to the motel lobby, leaving him to get back to work. Sighing, he walked to the back to see if he could convince one of the workers to help him with the crosses.

"Hey, Earl," he called out as he stepped around the corner. "You were right, sheriff's all in a lather. I was thinking we could set them back up at the base of the hill."

"Already ahead of ya, Mr. Tanner," Fred said as he moved to grab the last cross leaning against the building.

Robert nodded to the man and watched him walk to the end of the row of crosses set up to mirror how they were when they'd started building. *Well, further away from the corn.* Worry squirmed in his belly at the thought. The paperwork they received all those months ago specifically asked them to remove the crosses.

Also said to work with the sheriff … that's what I'm doing. Robert glanced at the other two men. They were quietly rushing to finish up. Earl was quite clear they would stop working today, forcing him to pay them twice as much as necessary to complete the job before the month ended. He walked around the property, making mental notes as he worked up his final checklist. Everything looked right; he just hoped they passed inspection from their mysterious benefactor.

He will be our first guest, and if all goes well … Robert couldn't finish the thought; it was too fantastical, too unbelievable. Yet, here he was in the middle of nowhere Texas doing the impossible for a chance to find out if it was true. He prayed to God it was, but something deep in his gut told him God had nothing to do with it.

CHAPTER FOUR

"Are those new?" Ruth asked as Robert stepped into the lobby.

He glanced out the window to catch several crows flying around and offered a shrug to his wife. "Honestly, I have no idea. I'd assume that horrifying scarecrow kept everything away, but maybe it only works on humans."

Ruth nodded and turned her attention back to the corn across the way. The ball of fear that had been stuck in her chest for the last few weeks slid down to her belly as she watched the crows hop about The Scarecrow's perch. She counted five so far but thought there might be a few more out of sight. They were larger than any crow she'd ever seen and darker than midnight.

The Scarecrow's dark eyes glittered in the s'tting sunlight. A gasp slipped from her lips, and her eyes widened. Robert followed her gaze to The Scarecrow. It seemed to be watching the motel, them in particular, with its cold black eyes. His mouth opened, but before he could say anything, the door opened. Earl stood nervously in the doorway.

"Mr. Tanner," he said in that way that excluded Ruth from the conversation, to her annoyance.

"What is it, Earl?"

"Mr. Tanner, work's all done. We'd like to scoot out of here before the sun sets."

"Sure, sure," he replied as he stepped to the counter and grabbed the envelope they had set aside for the men's pay. He walked to the door with Ruth in tow. Nathan and Fred stood with their heads down a few feet away. "Everything we agreed on is here, but I wanted to remind you we could still use some help. Twenty-five dollars a week and you can stay in one of the extra rooms."

"Thanks, but no thanks, Mr. Tanner," Earl said as he snatched the envelope away. "We really have to be goin'. Y'all will see soon enough."

Nathan offered a nod while Fred grumbled thanks as they turned to crawl into the back of Earl's wagon. The two horses snorted and stamped, eager to return home. As Earl took his seat, he stared at Robert for a moment before shaking his head and snapping his whip to get the horses moving.

"Make your peace tonight," he called out over his shoulder as the wagon pulled away.

"They have no idea," Ruth whispered, turning her attention back to the corn. The largest crow stood on the shoulder of The Scarecrow, one dark eye seemingly staring directly into her soul. "No idea."

CHAPTER FIVE

Orville rolled off the woman as the sun dipped lower and covered the grove in shadows. She struggled to push the dress over her groin with one hand as her other arm attempted to cover her breasts, the top half of the dress having been ripped in his excitement.

Won't matter soon. Orville's belly squirmed at the thought. Once the sun was down, he had a few hours tops to set the girl in place and hightail it out of there.

Sighing, he struggled to stand while pulling up his overalls. He hated this part; just handing them over. Yet he knew the consequences would be too great to ignore the deal he had in place with The Scarecrow.

He could always find another girl. They were a dime a dozen if you knew where to look.

He glanced down at the woman. Her body trembled as quiet tears ran from her eyes. She was older than the ones he usually took but almost as delicious. He smirked at the woman and squatted next to her. She flinched when he reached out, but he forgave her. He had been rougher than he planned to be that last time. He grew hard again as he thought of her cries.

No time for that. There was still too much work to do.

A crow cried out above, soon followed by more as they flew over the grove. They were warning him. *It's now or never.* Orville pressed his hand against her cheek. The woman shuddered as a sob ripped from her mouth. *They always know when it's over.*

"Now's not the time for makin' a fuss," he said as his hand slid up to her hair and made a fist.

She gasped when his grip tightened, pulling her hair away from the scalp. Orville stood, bringing the woman to her feet as well. Her hands were now locked on his wrist as she struggled to free herself. He lifted her from the ground and stared longingly at her breasts as the top of the sundress slid to bunch at her hips. They were larger than what he usually saw, making them a bit exotic. Another caw brought his attention back to the task at hand.

Orville reared back with his free arm and slammed his ham-sized fist into her face. There was a crunch as her nose flatted under his blow. She issued a squeak before going limp. He slung the woman over his shoulder and stomped from the grove.

He followed the dust kicked up by the wagon's retreat from the motel for a moment before walking down the hill. Purples, pinks, reds, and blues swirled together to darken the sky as the sun continued its path west. The crows flew overhead, dipping low to cry out. Sweat ran down his face and chest, and he struggled to catch his breath.

Orville was an enormous man, shaped almost like a box, with wide shoulders and hips and a massive amount of bulk filling him in. His light blonde hair was thinning, but he hated wearing hats because they trapped so much of the Texas heat. To keep cool, he wore nothing under his overalls. That and he enjoyed the feel of the rough material rubbing against his skin. He did make sure to have sturdy boots at all times and socks to match. *A strong foundation is crucial.*

Yet, even with the precautions, his bulk made any fast movement a struggle. *You can rest after.* The thought of The Scarecrow waking before he finished gave Orville all the persuasion needed to keep moving.

He passed the crosses that fella moved back from the corn and glanced at the motel. There was no one outside, and he studied the windows to make sure no one was watching. Wouldn't do to have some stranger try and stop him. There could be no disappointing The Scarecrow.

Orville entered the corn and slowed to a brisk walk. His breaths came in wheezing gasps, and his chest tightened sporadically. The woman shifted on his shoulder, and worry crept into his belly. He could feel it sloshing around inside him, and he knew without question if he wasn't careful, it would turn to fear quickly. He pushed ahead, moving from row to row, his eyes locked on The Scarecrow hovering over the sea of cornstalks.

The bag hanging from his belt jingled with each step. He concentrated on the sound, using it to set his pace. The Scarecrow grew closer, and soon, he stood under the thing. Four crows landed on the crossbeam and studied Orville. They stood quietly, staring until his skin crawled.

He looked up at The Scarecrow, and a shiver went down his back. It was not good to be here this close to the harvest. He let the woman tumble from his shoulder. She landed with a moan but otherwise lay still. He pulled a hammer and four iron train spikes from the bag. Sitting on her chest, he pinned her left arm to the ground before driving the iron spike through her wrist and into the hard soil.

A scream ripped from her lips as the spike drove deeper with each blow. The crows answered her cry with their own, creating a massive noise. Orville grew harder as he studied the pain flashing over her features. He moved to her right wrist, getting a louder scream from the woman. Her eyes rolled back, showing all whites as she squirmed beneath him. Desire flushed through his body, overwhelming the fear in his belly. *Is there time for one last go?*

The corn plunged into darkness as the sun finally set. Orville realized the time was up. The crows grew quiet as the woman stilled. Orville hoped this was enough. He stood, his head down, unable to look at The Scarecrow, and ran back through the corn. He wanted to be out before it was too late. Angling toward the house, he struggled to keep his breathing down.

A single, solitary caw sounded from behind, and then dry, dusty laughter chased after Orville through the corn. His manhood shriveled at the sound. A desperate sob built in his chest. He slapped his hand over his mouth, hoping to stifle the sound when it escaped.

"Run, child," the dry voice whispered on the wind. "Run and bring me another soul before the harvest ends."

CHAPTER SIX

"Did you hear that?" Robert asked as he looked up from dinner.

"Maybe one of those crows?"

"Maybe," he answered back to his wife, afraid to share what he thought it really might be.

Robert returned his attention to the half-eaten sandwich on his plate. His stomach rolled with unease, and he pushed the plate away. Ruth reached over and took his hand with a squeeze. He glanced up and offered her a smile, but she was staring blankly ahead, lost in her thoughts.

She's still the most beautiful woman I've ever laid eyes on. His smile slipped at the thought, not because it wasn't true but because of how much the last eleven months had worn on them. Robert couldn't remember the last time he studied his own face in the mirror, but he was sure he didn't wear the tragedy near as well as his wife.

Her once smooth skin carried subtle signs of constant worry, and her golden hair held a bit more silver. Her eyes no longer twinkled in excitement and wonder, instead reflecting only unease and loss. Yet she still took his breath away when he really took the time to see her.

"I love you," he whispered, throat suddenly tight.

Ruth blinked before turning her stare in his direction. She studied his face, and the corners of her lips turned up ever so slightly. She squeezed his hand once more before pulling away. His heart sank as she stood and quietly collected the plates.

What did you expect? He hadn't said those words to her since the funeral. Not because he blamed her or had ever stopped loving her, but because he wasn't sure love existed anymore. Yet, still, he held those words away from her, so much so Ruth stopped saying it as well. For months, both kept the one thing they both desperately needed away from each other, and in the process, their hearts hardened.

Robert only hoped it wasn't too late. If tomorrow worked ... if the man delivered what he promised, how could it be?

The Scarecrow studied the woman as she breathed. *The child is growing ... in size and appetites.* There was a time it might have appreciated the beauty of the woman before it, but now, after so many years, it was looking for two things. Glancing to the sky, it stared at the half-moon, excited to see it high above.

A groan pulled his attention back to the woman. Her eyes were wide, shining with terror. The Scarecrow gripped his scythe's handle and stepped from his perch, landing with a thump. The woman twisted and thrashed, trying to free herself from the iron spikes but instead soaking the ground with more of her blood.

Its head leaned back as if taking in a deep whiff of air. *Yes, there it is.* It stepped to the woman and leaned over, gripping her long hair in a balled fist. She cried out, first for help, then simply screaming as The Scarecrow ripped her from the iron spikes. Blood sprayed from her wrists as her screams intensified with the pain. The sound washed over The Scarecrow, and he swelled with excitement.

It studied her for a moment, her body bathed in the red. It pulled back the scythe and swung, slicing easily through her neck. The body tumbled to the ground as blood sprayed from the newly formed stump. The Scarecrow held the head over its own and let the blood soak into its burlap skin.

The largest crow landed on The Scarecrow's shoulder, pressing its beak against the strawman's cheek. They absorbed all the blood, gaining strength with each drop. The other crows began their cries as they flew down onto the discarded corpse.

"Yesss," The Scarecrow said, its body humming with newfound energy. "The harvest has begun."

Sheriff Pike stared at his two deputies, who were standing on the other side of his desk. This was the first harvest with an outsider on the force. Not his choice, but apparently, someone in the Governor's office pulled some strings. *What's done is done.*

"Deputy Boyle," he said with a smile, "I need you to head out tomorrow morning to the new motel and check on our newest residents, the Tanners."

"Are you sure?" Deputy Smite blurted out.

Pike glared at the man, aware that Boyle was watching his fellow deputy from the corner of his eye. "I don't know Smite … am I sure?"

"Sorry, sir," Smite said, his head hanging low, "just surprised."

"Well, the best way for Boyle to understand the area is to dive in head first. You all right with that?" Pike asked, swinging his attention to Boyle.

"Yes, sir," Boyle said with a puzzled look. "Honestly, I don't understand all the hullabaloo. I've been here about six months, and it's been fairly quiet."

"You will," Pike said as he waved the two men from his office. "You will."

CHAPTER SEVEN

Orville stumbled from the cornfield at a run until his feet struck the newly paved road. He stopped and turned back in time to see The Scarecrow step from its perch and disappear into the stalks. Swinging his attention to the motel, he glared at the new building. That had almost cost him his life. He'd never have waited so long if so many people hadn't been around.

His throat grew tight as he wondered what might have 'appened if The Scarecrow had awoken without a sacrifice ready. *Who is foolish enough to build so close to the corn?* He stepped as quietly as his bulk would allow and moved to get a closer look.

Voices drew him to the first window on the west side of the building. Orville stood in the dark a few feet away and watched a woman carry two plates to the counter and place them down. She stared out into the night, and for a moment, his stomach squirmed in fear.

The woman was old, well, older than most he took the time to study. Her hair was shoulder-length and not yet ready to give up on being blonde. He liked how the two colors seemed to interweave to form a lighter golden-like color. He thought her pretty, but her real beauty shone in the sadness reflected in her eyes. His heart began to beat faster as he imagined her underneath him, open and inviting him to enter.

The woman sighed, turned, and disappeared from his sight. A moment later, a light popped on and shined through the next window. Orville stepped over, delighted when the woman slid into sight. His breath caught as she stood bare from the waist up in front of a shelf and mirror.

She rubbed a washcloth against a bar of soap in the basin on the shelf. His gaze locked onto the cloth, following it up to her skin where she began to wash. Orville released tiny panting breaths as her breasts bounced with the motion. Although it was a typical hot night, her nipples were hard—likely from the cool water, he imagined.

His hand reached down and rubbed the coarse material against his stiffening penis. He'd never experienced such sexual excitement from a woman before. He prayed she'd push her dress further down as he rubbed faster on the front of his overalls. She froze when a moan slipped from his lips. Her head turned towards the open window, searching into the darkness.

Orville shuddered when their eyes locked, unable to stop himself from ejaculating. She screamed, throwing her arm across her bare breasts, and rushed out of view. A man's voice spoke, but Orville couldn't make it out over the woman's cries. He spun and ran towards the crosses. If he made it to the crosses, he'd be safe.

As he ran, more screams came, from the corn this time. The only safe place was on the other side of the crosses if The Scarecrow had begun the harvest. *Only a fool would be out here now.* An icy ball of fear grew in his belly at the thought. He began to run faster. He was a lot of things, but a fool wasn't one of them.

CHAPTER EIGHT

Robert threw the door open to their bedroom. Ruth rushed towards him, burying her face into his chest as he wrapped his arms around her.

"What is it?" he asked as she broke down into tears.

"Someone was watching me," she managed to say through choking sobs.

He held her out, grabbed the top of her dress from her waist, and slid it back up.

"Wait here," he said, then spun and ran to grab his shotgun from the rack on the wall and a flashlight from the shelf.

Robert ran out the door and around to the side of the building, swinging the light back and forth as he searched for the Peeping Tom.

Cries of help came from behind, and he turned towards the corn as a bone-chilling shriek sounded. He froze when he saw several crows pass through his light and descend into the corn.

"Robert?"

He turned his head toward Ruth where she leaned out their bathroom window. "I don't know," he said.

"Please, just come inside. Tomorrow is too important, let's go to bed."

Robert nodded. "All right. I'll be there in a moment."

He waited for her to disappear back into the house before turning back to the field. If he wanted any chance at sleep, he needed to know. His first step was hesitant, as if his body was fighting him from moving forward. Gritting his teeth, he took another step, then another, until he was running over the road.

Robert slid to a stop at the edge of the corn. This was as close to the field as he'd ever stepped. His body began to tremble, there was a looseness in his gut, and he knew if he waited too much longer, he wouldn't be able to move. Terror washed over him, increasing the tremors and drying his mouth.

He chambered a shell; the familiar sound of the pump-action calming him a bit. *Whatever is out there, this will take care of it.* Robert stepped into the corn, holding his flashlight against the side of the barrel. The sounds of the crows drew him deeper into the field. The light from the half-moon above and his own flashlight helped him navigate through the stalks.

Robert stepped into a clearing and froze. His light fell on The Scarecrow, standing at the base of its perch. A woman's head dangled from its hand. A weird slash of light hung in the air next to The Scarecrow. The sounds of feeding pulled his attention and his light to a pile of crows fighting over what Robert assumed was the rest of the woman.

Bile burned his throat, and he spewed vomit onto the ground. Dry laughter filled his ears as he locked eyes with the of The Scarecrow. The light from the flashlight illuminated its face, gleaming off its dark eyes. Thick brown lips curled into a smile as The Scarecrow tossed the head into the light.

"A fruitful beginning to this harvest," it said.

Robert pulled the trigger and stumbled back. Loud, angry cries came from the crows as he turned and blindly ran toward the motel. Laughter followed him through the corn, driving him faster until he burst out of the stalks and tumbled to the edge of the road. Scrambling to his feet, Robert saw Ruth standing by their door.

"Get inside," he hollered as he began to run again.

Ruth stood frozen for a moment, then her eyes grew wide, and she darted back into the motel. Robert fought the urge to glance back, praying for the speed to make it inside unharmed.

What have we done?

The laughter grew louder as he slammed their door and turned the lock.

CHAPTER NINE

Ruth stared at the ceiling. It took almost half their only bottle of whisky, but Robert was finally asleep. She tried to make sense of his rambling but failed. Of course, nothing made sense anymore, not since that day. Ruth chewed absentmindedly on her bottom lip. If what was promised was delivered tomorrow, it would all be worthwhile.

Yet, she knew in her heart what was promised was impossible. Tomorrow would come, and once again, her heart would shatter. She glanced at her husband as he began to snore softly. Her eyes welled with tears. He had sacrificed everything for a chance to reunite their family on nothing but her word.

Her breath caught. It wasn't her word but his love for her that gave him the strength, she suddenly realized. *Will it be enough?* She'd never seen him as shook up as he was coming back from the corn tonight, not even on the day of the accident. Ruth wondered what could be worse than that day.

Nothing.

Her eyes closed as exhaustion finally won out against her nervous excitement of what tomorrow would bring. Her breathing slowed, and she snuggled deeper into her pillow. Tomorrow, her family would be together again. The Pale Man had promised.

Robert's eyes popped open. *What was that?* He was sure he heard something … maybe in a dream? He struggled to remember, but such activity seemed to only make his head ache more. The cornfield flashed in his mind, and he groaned, suddenly grateful he couldn't remember his dreams.

There. Robert sat up, glancing at his wife. She continued to sleep, to no surprise. She always was a heavy sleeper. He swung his legs off the bed and sat for a moment, waiting to hear the sound again. Standing, he crept to the door that led to their kitchen and dining room. He pulled the door open and peeked through the crack.

"Why, Robert, no reason to sneak around your own home," the man sitting at his table said. He gestured to the other chair before filling two glasses with some of the whiskey Robert hadn't consumed.

Robert eyed the shotgun on the rack as he stepped into the room, gently closing the door behind him. The man was abnormally long and looked out of place sitting in their chair. His long dark hair emphasized just how pale his skin was in the brightly lit room. Robert moved to the open seat.

"My gift to you," the man said as he took a sip from his glass. "The motel is on a very special piece of land, and since you followed the plans I provided, you will reap the rewards."

Robert wrapped his hands around his glass, unsure what to say. He'd thought it foolish to wire the building for electricity when it was obvious the company had no plans in providing them any when they applied for the permits, but Ruth insisted that it must be followed to a T.

"Yes, Mrs. Tanner can be quite persuasive when she wants something," the Pale Man said, a sly smile on his lips.

Robert stared at the man. Something was off, but he couldn't place it.

"Why are you here?"

"To complete our bargain, of course," he said as he swirled the amber liquid in his glass.

"Is she here?" Robert whispered, his heart suddenly hammering against his chest.

"Not yet, but soon," The Pale Man replied. "Just as soon as we finish the paperwork."

The Pale Man reached into his jacket and pulled out a rolled-up piece of parchment secured with a black ribbon. He placed it at the center of the table. Robert stared at the paper a moment before reaching out and sliding it closer. The Pale Man flashed a smile, then took another drink.

Robert pulled the ribbon and unrolled the paper.

"I don't read ... what is this, Latin?"

"Close," The Pale Man said. "It is a simple contract. You agree to take care of this place until such time as you cannot continue, and I will deliver the promised item at the beginning. If you prefer, I can have your wife sign it."

A chill ran through Robert. He glanced up, locking eyes with The Pale Man. Neither blinked as the silence stretched. He jumped when a tapping sounded at the window, then he focused back on The Pale Man, who now held out a pen. Robert grabbed it and scribbled his name on the line at the bottom.

"Very good, Mr. Tanner," The Pale Man said. He finished his drink. "Tomorrow at dusk, you will find the desired prize."

The tapping sounded again. Robert stood, tentatively stepping to the window. His fingers gripped the curtain, but he held still as his insides turned to ice. He waited until the tapping repeated before pulling back the curtain.

A large crow stood on the sill and periodically struck its beak against the glass. In the moonlight, Robert could see The Scarecrow standing a few feet away. Raspy laughter flittered into the room as the crow began to cry out, striking its wings against the glass.

Robert stumbled back, his feet tangling up. His head struck the edge of the table, and his world went black.

CHAPTER TEN

"Robert," Ruth said as she gently shook his shoulder. "Wake up."

His eyes fluttered open with a groan, and the sunlight nearly blinded him. His head pounded, and when he ran his hand through his hair, he found a lump on the back of his head. *The dream … or was it real?*

"Is she …" he trailed off, afraid to know the truth.

"No, the sheriff sent a deputy to check on us," she said with wide eyes.

Robert bolted up. *The Scarecrow killed that girl in the field.* His stomach rolled as he staggered from the bedroom.

The deputy glanced up from the bottle of whisky in his hand. He placed the bottle on the table and turned his full attention to Robert.

"Deputy …?"

"Boyle, Mr. Tanner."

"Deputy Boyle, something happened last night …" he said before dropping his voice to a whisper, "in the corn."

Robert continued past the man, afraid if he stopped, he might never move again. His head pounded with each step. The deputy sighed behind him before following him outside.

"Are you sure you didn't mean in the wheat?" Boyle asked as he stopped next to Robert, who stood by the road.

Robert ignored the man, his eyes locked on The Scarecrow hanging from his perch, as it had the entire time the motel was being built. Sunlight glinted from the dark stone eyes, which seemed to be staring straight at them. Several crows perched across its arms, picking at their feathers or rubbing their beaks against one another. Letting out a deep breath, Robert marched across the road.

"Mr. Tanner," Boyle hollered.

"I didn't drink until after I saw …" again he trailed off, unsure exactly what to believe. The man at the table flashed in his head with the signed contract. *That was just a dream … right?*

Robert entered the corn, pushing past the stalks until he found a row. Angry caws sounded as he made his way towards The Scarecrow's perch. His eyes glanced down every so often for any signs of what he thought happened the night before.

"Goddamn it," Boyle growled from behind. "Do you not understand? It's not safe for your wife to have you slip into the bottle."

The deputy moved up next to him and matched his stride, but Robert almost felt the man willing him to hurry up. An icy ball formed once again, sending chills throughout his body. His skin crawled as the crows began to cry louder. Boyle's head was up, tracking the birds as they took to the sky and lazily circled overhead. They entered the clearing below where The Scarecrow rested.

"See," Robert said, excited to find the blood on the ground. "Proof."

"Of what, exactly?" Boyle asked as he stood on the edge.

"It killed a girl last night," Robert said as he stepped closer to the center, looking for the body. "Cut her head clean off."

"It?" Boyle repeated after a moment of silence. "Jesus, you mean the scarecrow?"

"Well ... yeah," he replied as he clapped his hands in excitement. Pointing into the corn stalks, he exclaimed, "There, there she is. I knew it."

Boyle took a deep breath and walked to the area Robert pointed towards. There was a bloody mess piled together and partially hidden by the stalks. He squatted down and sighed, then stood, holding out the remains of a rabbit.

"Looks like the crows made a mess of the poor guy."

"But ..." Robert glanced up at The Scarecrow. *Was it a dream? All of it?*

"Can we please head back to the motel?" Boyle asked as he flung the remains into the corn. "This place still gives me the creeps."

Robert followed him, shuffling behind while trying to understand what had happened the night before. He barked out in pain as his foot came down onto something sharp. Hopping on one foot for a moment, he held the other and stared at the deep gouge on the pad of his foot. Blood welled up and dripped to the ground to be soaked up by the soil.

He studied the ground, hoping to find what he stepped on, but the impatient call of the deputy pulled his attention back to the motel. Gritting his teeth, he placed the injured foot down and shambled after the man as quickly as it would allow. Robert glanced back one last time and gasped. A huge crow pecked into the earth. As it pulled its beak up, it held a portion of a femur bone, one end bright red with blood.

CHAPTER ELEVEN

Ruth was standing in the parking lot when they stepped out from the field. Robert glanced at her fists pressed against her hips and fought the urge to groan. Ignoring the pain of every step, he rushed past the deputy and stopped in front of his wife. She studied him in silence until the deputy was close by.

"Well?"

Robert flinched, unsure what to say, so he chose to say nothing.

"Looks like some poor critter got ganged up on by those crows," Boyle said after a brief pause.

"You sure it wasn't that big fella?" she asked, staring daggers at her husband.

"I'm sorry, what?"

"He didn't tell ya?" Ruth asked with a deepening scowl. "There was somebody out here last night, watching me through the bathroom window. Robert chased him off."

Boyle turned his attention to her husband, who, after a moment, nodded and said, "We heard screaming from the corn."

"I'm not sure what we heard, Deputy," Ruth said, her unblinking eyes locked with her husband's.

"Probably an animal; out here in the dark, it's hard to tell the difference sometimes."

Robert opened his mouth to argue but froze as Ruth's right eyebrow rose. He swallowed, instead offering a noncommittal shrug. His injured foot throbbed, and soon his head pounded in rhythm. He lifted the foot off the ground, letting it hover over the warming asphalt.

"Even so," Ruth countered, "that man was real enough. Built like a box and as large as a Longhorn."

Boyle nodded. "Okay … I'll look in on the usual suspects. If you see him again, let us know." He tipped the brim of his hat and stepped quickly to his car.

Robert closed his eyes as he listened to the car start up and drive away. Sweat ran down his face and back as the sun began to beat down on them. Ruth slipped closer, pressing her palm against his forehead.

"You're in no shape for tonight," she barked, looping her arm through his and guiding him back to their room.

Robert began to hop on his good foot while holding the injured foot above the carpet. Now was not the time to make any more mess. She helped him to the bedroom and let go so he could flop onto the bed with a groan. Ruth rushed to the bathroom and returned with their first-aid kit.

"Now listen here," she said as she treated the cut, "you will not go to the corn again. Do you understand?"

He nodded, not willing to extend the argument any length. His head throbbed and soon hurt more than the foot. He needed to rest, to get ready for the big night. Ruth finished wrapping his foot and stepped to the side of the bed. He refused to open his eyes, simply mouthing thanks before slipping back into sleep.

CHAPTER TWELVE

Ruth stared down at her husband. He'd never been one to drink to excess. *Whatever he saw out there in the corn weren't no animal.* Of that, she was sure. *Or that mountain of a man either.* Oh, Ruth was sure he played some part in it, but he was long gone when Robert stepped onto the field.

The last time she'd seen him so shook up was right after the accident, and even then, he just cried himself to sleep. He hadn't touched a drop of that devil water for years and then practically drowned himself in it after his trip to the corn. She ran her finger across his forehead, sweeping back the loose hair. Tonight would show him it was all worthwhile. If the man in her dreams was real, and there wasn't any reason to disbelieve him now, then their family would be back together.

They'd just have to avoid the corn, and once they'd paid the man's asking price, they could move far away.

She shuffled to the front, leaving Robert to rest up. Glancing around the room, her eyes fell upon the bottle. A flash of heat surged through her. She stomped over and snatched it up, marched to the sink, and poured out the contents.

Ruth carried the empty bottle outside and walked to the side of the road. She glared at The Scarecrow and the crows resting across its arms. Its black eyes glinted in the sunlight. The crows began to cry out, their caws piercing the silence. She'd have to see why they couldn't just take the perch down. *Not sure I can live here with those eyes staring at us every minute.*

"Not like it actually works," she mumbled as she reared back with the bottle and flung it towards The Scarecrow.

The largest crow burst into the air, catching the bottle and dropping it to shatter on the road below. Ruth stared at the bird circling lazily above her until the caws of the other birds pulled her attention back to the perch.

A shiver ran down her spine as she locked eyes with The Scarecrow. Its left eye winked. A startled gasp slipped from Ruth as she stumbled backward before spinning and running to the motel. Dry, raspy laughter followed her on the breeze, chasing her through the parking lot and only stopping when she slammed the door shut.

CHAPTER THIRTEEN

Deputy Boyle sat in his police cruiser. It was one of the perks he enjoyed since joining the force. Another one was getting to put trash in their place, trash like Orville Perkins. He studied the man's house with disgust. *How can a person live like this?* Large piles of refuse surrounded the small shack, leaving Boyle to wonder if they might be the only things holding the walls up.

The lone window's curtain fluttered. *Ah, so the man is home.* Boyle slipped from his car and marched to the front door. He hesitated a moment, glancing around as if to make sure the man wouldn't materialize out of thin air. As he pulled back his fist to hammer on the door, it opened to a grinning Orville.

"Just hate when a boil pops up without warning," he said, stepping out and closing the door behind him. "I never know if I'm supposed to squish it right away or wait until it's big enough to lance."

Boyle's jaw clenched as he fought the urge to pull out his nightstick and start beating on the man. Instead, he locked eyes with the oversized simpleton. Sweat beaded on Orville's forehead and ran down into his eyes. His smile grew less and less with every heartbeat until his lips sat in a slight frown.

"Mrs. Tanner claims you were peeping last night," Boyle finally said just as Orville began to open his mouth to speak.

The man's lips pressed together, the frown deepening, and he crossed his bare arms across his chest. "Weren't me."

"Right … like anyone else in a hundred miles fits the description she gave of the pervert."

Orville's eyes squinched up at the last word. His arms unfolded, slipping to his sides, and his hands balled into fists. Boyle blinked, his expression one of unconcern. He learned long ago to never show these bumpkins any sign of fear. They could smell it quicker than a coon dog.

"Weren't me," Orville said again, each word practically spat out. The muscles in his neck bulged, and his entire body seemed to tense.

"Don't do anything stupid," Boyle said, his voice dropping the temperature between them.

Orville relaxed, holding his hands up with the palms out. Boyle grimaced at the gunk and grime collected all over the man's skin.

"No matter how dumb y'all think I am, I ain't dumb enough to be on that side of the crosses during harvest season. Hell, that sucker pushed them even farther out."

"Well, keep it that way," Boyle said as he stepped backward toward his cruiser. "I don't want to hear you've been anywhere near that motel, you hear?"

"Ain't no fool," Orville called out, flashing a black-toothed grin.

Boyle nodded slowly. It was only the second time he'd been this close to the man, but he was beginning to see the truth. Orville Perkins only acted this way to distract from something much darker.

CHAPTER FOURTEEN

Sheriff Pike sat in front of his office's new oscillating fan. He stared blankly at the wall, the previous night's dream replaying in his head.

The Pale Man was standing next to his wife's side of the bed, bent so close he could kiss her cheek. When he noticed Pike standing in the doorway, he winked, then pressed his extraordinarily long finger to his lips when Pike opened his mouth.

Pike blinked; the two men now stood face to face in his office. The Pale Man flashed a smile, the kind of smile that guilty people who routinely got away with it wore.

"Sheriff," he said in that quiet voice of his, "I just wanted to remind you what is at stake as the harvest approaches. Do not do anything silly just because the motel is finished. I still need you to work hand in hand with the Tanners to deliver what I expect … what I require."

Pike glared at the man, wishing to return to the time before he ever heard of Donn, Texas. His wife's sleeping face flashed in his head, and he sighed. For her, he would do anything, and that was exactly what he did all those years ago.

The Pale Man had come to him and offered a chance at saving his wife's life.

Pike struck a bargain, one he barely understood or truly believed, but once they arrived, Beth no longer experienced the symptoms of her cancer. There was a twist, of course; dealings like this always contained fine print. While she no longer needed treatment or suffered from the cancer itself, her body stayed the same as the first day they arrived in town. Always so prideful of her appearance, Pike knew it killed her to still appear sick.

It's in the past. He clung to that thought, pushing out those memories that made him want to press his gun to his forehead and pull the trigger. There was too much at stake, and like it or not, Pike was well aware of his responsibilities. *Damn him.* A knock pulled his attention to his door.

"Sheriff?" Boyle asked as he hovered in the doorway, only entering once Pike nodded. "The Tanners experienced a bit of a scare last night."

He fought the urge to reply with *you don't say*, instead just motioning for the man to continue.

"Orville Perkins was peeping on Mrs. Tanner," he said with a frown. "He swears it wasn't him, but no one matches the description she gave me better. Everyone knows Perkins is a pervert."

"That's true, but his tastes usually run much younger," Pike replied as he stood up, his daughter's face flashing before him. Grimacing, he patted Boyle on the shoulder. "We'll just have to keep a closer eye on our boy Orville. So … nothing else?"

"Other than Mr. Tanner mistaking a crow kill for a murder? Not much."

Sheriff Pike studied Boyle in silence just long enough for it to grow uncomfortable. Boyle was new to the force and, more importantly, not from around the area. He balked at anything out of the ordinary, but Pike knew he would come around. It only took one harvest to become a believer. The sheriff forced a smile on his lips. "Good job."

CHAPTER FIFTEEN

"Mrs. Tanner?"

Ruth swung her attention from The Scarecrow to the man walking up the road. He was familiar, but she was struggling to place why. *Is he one of Earl's workers?* She nodded at the thought and waited for him to move closer. The man walked at a quick pace, with a bundle over his right shoulder. The cloth bulged in places, and Ruth wondered if it contained his every possession.

"I'm not sure you remember me," the man said as he pulled up a few feet from her, wearing a crooked grin.

She assumed he meant it to be disarming, but goosebumps popped up on her arms.

"You were here with Earl," she said, struggling to keep a tremor from her voice.

"Yes, ma'am, my name is Nathan Ray," he said, pulling his hat from his head with his free hand. He studied the ground as he continued. "Well, I was hoping the offer Mr. Tanner extended might still be available?"

Ruth relaxed, the sudden burst of fear gone, and after a moment, she nodded. "Yes, sir. The motel is open, and hopefully, we'll have guests sooner than later. Give me a moment and I'll grab you a key."

The smile returned to Nathan's face, this time lighting up his eyes as well.

Ruth shook her head, unsure why she was so scared just moments ago. The man seemed pleasant enough. She disappeared into the lobby, returning a few minutes later holding a room key.

"I assume I don't have to give you the grand tour," she said as she handed it to him.

"No, ma'am. I truly am grateful for this," he said, putting his hat back on his head. "After I put my stuff down, is there anything you need me to do?"

Ruth bit her bottom lip in thought. "I guess just check all the rooms to make sure they're ready ... then give the garden a quick look-see."

"Yes, ma'am."

Ruth stared at his back as he hurried to his room, number eight. She always thought it odd how small they were told to build the place but was happy it wasn't any bigger. Even with the new help, the place was going to be difficult to keep up, but it was worth it if the man in her dreams was telling her the truth. She turned her attention back to the cornfield and The Scarecrow as tears leaked from her eyes.

CHAPTER SIXTEEN

Orville scratched at his crotch, bringing his fingers up to sniff. *Whoo-wee, I'm getting ripe.* He sat on the front steps, avoiding the stifling heat inside. Maybe a walk over to the pond was just what he needed. Standing, he stretched, arching his back until he received a satisfying pop.

"Shit," he mumbled as the sheriff's car pulled to a stop a few feet away. His jaw clenched a moment, then he took a deep breath to relax and smiled wide. "Twice in one day, I've never felt so much love."

Pike stepped from his cruiser and leaned against the door. He studied Orville, letting the silence stretch on until Orville couldn't take it anymore.

"Whatcha want, boss man?" he asked as he stepped toward the sheriff. The last thing he wanted was anyone snooping around his place. *Best to keep the fuzz as far away as possible.*

"Orville Perkins, you best stay away from that new motel," Pike said before turning his head to spit. "I have enough of a headache with those outsiders living next to the corn. I don't need you trying to stick your pecker in Ruth Tanner as well."

Ruth Tanner? His penis shifted as he put a name to the image of her bare chest and golden hair. A soft moan sounded from the back of his throat as he pictured his hands sliding over her soft skin. A jolt of pain shattered his fantasy as he found himself laying face first on the dirt road.

The sheriff drove his knee into his back and pushed up on his arm, causing Orville to squeal.

"I'm serious, you vile piece of shit," Pike said through gritted teeth. "Nobody's gonna give a good goddamn if you up and disappear. Stay away from the Tanners and you may live to see the end of the harvest season."

Orville grunted as the sheriff released him and stood up. He fought the urge to roll over and kick out at the man, instead lying completely still as Pike cocked his firearm. He rolled to his side once the sheriff's footsteps quieted and the car turned over. The sheriff did a quick turn, blowing dust over Orville and sending him into a coughing fit.

We'll see who lasts the season.

Sheriff Pike pulled into the motel's parking lot. He shook his head, still in disbelief there was a building where just a few weeks ago there was only grass and crosses. Anger flared as he glanced around, unable to find the crosses from his vehicle. He slid out, slamming his door to announce himself in case the car itself hadn't made enough noise. He stomped to the edge of the road and stared at The Scarecrow.

"Sheriff?"

Pike turned his attention to Mrs. Tanner as she walked towards him. He nodded and met her halfway, not comfortable being that close to the corn. *Shit, back in my office isn't far enough away.* There was a worried look on her face, and Pike sighed, taking off his hat.

"I spoke with who we believe was your Peeping Tom. He denies it, but I made it clear what would happen if he returns. Just let us know if you see him again," Pike said in a rush. He wasn't too comfortable talking about it with this slip of a woman.

"Thank you," Ruth said, her lips frozen in a half-smile. "He just startled me is all."

"Well, Orville has been known to startle most people, ma'am. Your husband around?"

She shook her head, her eyes darting over his shoulder at the corn and then returning to the sheriff's face. "He suffered quite the scare last night and had a bit too much to drink. He's sleeping it off. Can I help ya?"

Pike ran his hat's brim through his fingers, turning the thing while he thought a moment. He was reluctant to discuss this with the woman, but after a deep breath, he simply said, "The crosses, ma'am."

"They're around back a bit," she said, pointing with a nod of her head. "Richard asked the workers to put them back up. I know it's not exactly how they were, but we didn't want to scare off travelers."

Pike slipped his hat back on and started to walk to the end of the motel." If you don't mind, I'll have a look-see and then head out."

Ruth didn't answer as he walked away and disappeared around the corner. He slowed when a whistling sounded up ahead. His hand slid to his holster, stopping to rest on his revolver's handle. Stepping lightly, he peeked around the corner to the back of the building.

"Jesus, Nathan," Pike said, barking a laugh. "You scared the shit out of me."

"Sorry, Sheriff," the man replied as he rocked back to his knees, his fist closed around a bunch of weeds. "Mrs. Tanner hired me on to help look after the place."

Pike stared at the man a moment, concern on his face. Nathan wasn't a stranger to the area. *Hell, he's been here longer than I have … he knows better.*

"I know what ya thinkin'," Nathan said as he stood, brushing at the dirt on his pants. "But times are tough, and the Tanners are still here … figured they made a deal to make this place safe. Got nothin' else to lose."

Pike reached out and rested his hand on Nathan's shoulder. He locked eyes with the man, and after a moment, gave a nod. Times were tougher, that was no lie, but seemed times were always tough for Nathan.

"Just be careful," Pike finally said as he pulled his hand away. "First sign of trouble, haul ass to those crosses."

"Well shit, Charles," he replied with a chuckle, "I didn't know you cared."

Pike tipped the brim of his hat in an exaggerated fashion and continued on, noting the crosses were indeed up but nowhere close to the property.

You'd have to really be moving to make it there if something was chasing you. Maybe Nathan was right, it might be the dawn of a new day.

Deep down, he knew it was wishful thinking. For as long as The Pale Man visited his dreams, Pike knew there would always be blood and death here.

CHAPTER SEVENTEEN

Ruth studied the sign she held in her hands. She'd asked Earl to paint the words on a scrap piece of black sheet metal. *Welcome weary traveler. Your journey nears its end.* She hoped it was the truth, but the longer the day dragged on, the gloomier she became. She hung the sign in the window and sighed. *Does it matter if it is?*

She guessed not and stepped outside to stare at the corn. Something was pulling at her, and she struggled to stay put. Her eyes studied The Scarecrow standing just above the corn. The crows circled over the field, taking turns to land on The Scarecrow and his perch. They issued their cries, often over each other, and Ruth wondered if they were talking to one another or to The Scarecrow.

The largest bird flew across the new road and landed in front of her. It didn't move any closer, just stared at her with one shiny black eye. She stared back at the creature, unsure what else she could do. The crow tilted its head, its beak opening wide but staying silent. Her heart raced, pounding against her chest like a drum roll.

What does it want?

"They act weird out here," Nathan said, standing at the corner of the building. "You want me to rush it?"

Ruth shook her head, unsure what the man even meant. These birds didn't seem all that fazed by humans. She glanced back to the corn and gasped.

The Scarecrow was gone.

"Nathan …" she managed to say his name before falling silent as she pointed to the corn.

He glanced there and froze. Ruth studied his face, aware he not only understood what she was referencing but that it terrified him. He stepped backward, his eyes never moving from the corn as he angled toward her.

"Mrs. Tanner," he whispered, flinching with each word. "We best get inside. It's not safe out here."

She nodded, moving her attention back to the corn as the stalks began to shake. Hoarse laughter issued from across the street. Her mouth went dry as the crow mimicked the laughter with its high-pitched call. She stumbled, causing her feet to tangle together and send her to the asphalt. The wind rushed from her lungs, leaving her gasping for breath. Nathan was at her side in a flash, babbling about getting inside.

The laughter grew in volume as the corn shook harder.

Ruth could see it swaying in a pattern as if someone was walking through the field. *Through the corn and towards us.* That icy ball of fear returned to her belly at the thought. Nathan scooped her up in his arms and hurried to the lobby. The crow issued one last cry before springing into the air to land on the corner of the roof.

Ruth finally caught her breath, gasping in fresh air while she stared at the bird. It hopped from one foot to the other like a child too excited to stay still. It issued a final cry as Nathan carried her inside the motel, slamming the lobby door behind him.

He immediately put her down and backed a few steps away with his hands up. "Ma'am, I was wrong."

Ruth shook her head. "No, it's okay. You were trying to help. My fool self stood frozen to the spot."

"Not that," he barked, eyes wide. "It's still happening, and we can't be here while it's hunting."

A thump sounded at the door, followed by another against the wall, and another farther down still until the thumping was continuous for half a minute.

A sudden silence fell over the motel, and Nathan slumped to the floor, covering his face with his hands. Ruth crept to the door, peeking out the slim window where her new sign hung.

A gasp slipped from her lips as she began to count the number of dead crows littering the parking lot. She stopped when she hit double digits and after glancing back at Nathan, who now rocked slightly back and forth, slowly turned the knob.

Ruth paused with the door just cracked open and waited a full minute before opening it wider. A caw sounded from off in the distance, and she tensed in case she needed to quickly close the door. It grew quiet once again, and then, so soft she wondered if it was her imagination, she heard a young girl cry out.

Swinging the door wide, Ruth stepped out and closed her eyes, focusing all her attention to listen for the girl. A soft breeze blew through the stalks, across the road, and over Ruth as she stood still. *There.* Her eyes popped open, and she rushed toward the corn. She was sure of it this time; there was a little girl out in that field, a little girl calling for her momma.

CHAPTER EIGHTEEN

Orville crouched in the tall grass by the pond a little way from his shack. He came to hop in the water and wash off the previous day's activities and cool down a bit. He spent the whole walk over planning the sheriff's death, but once he arrived, he found himself nothing but grateful for the delay.

Bell-like laughter stopped him from barging straight into the water; instead, he snuck up to the edge of the tall grass. A young couple stood in the middle of the pond, kissing passionately. He stared at the man's waist, excited to see a dainty pair of arms break from the water's surface and wrap around him. *Turn around.* The two broke off their kiss, the laughter coming again as the man placed his kisses onto her neck.

Orville's breath caught as the man's head slid out of the way and revealed the most beautiful creature he'd ever laid eyes on. Her wavy blonde hair was short, just past the jawline, and parted in the middle. It framed her face, highlighting her delicate features. Her lips were full, red, and rounded like those of the dolly his sister used to have.

The woman's eyes closed before her head flung back; tiny moans of pleasure slipped out of her mouth as the man's kisses slid from her neck down to her breasts. She pressed his face against her flesh in encouragement. Orville imagined she was pushing on the back of *his* head, and he grew aroused by her trembling form. He glanced around but found no one around save those two.

A loud gasp pulled his attention back to the couple. The man held her with one arm, the other under the water and out of Orville's sight.

What in tarnation is going on?

His excitement outgrew his frustration as his imagination filled in the details. The woman leaned into the man, her lips sucking on his shoulder before slipping to his neck. They began to slide through the water away from Orville and his hiding spot.

Orville unclasped his overalls, letting them fall to the ground. He kicked off his boots and rushed forward. The woman issued a yelp of surprise as water rained down on the couple from his entry into the pond. Orville grabbed the man by the hair, slammed his fist into his face, then dunked his head under the water.

Screaming, the woman splashed backward, scrambling to escape out of the water. Orville let out a whistle of appreciation as her breasts bounced up and down from the motion. He ignored the blows from the man, which grew softer with each second he was under the water's surface. The girl continued to scream but stopped moving once at the water's edge.

"Don't be shy, girl," Orville said with a hoot. "We gonna become the best of friends, just you wait."

Whimpering, she hugged her chest to cover her nipples. He pulled the man from the water and gave him a shake. Orville stepped closer, laughing as he tossed the man's still body up on the grass.

"Don't you worry your pretty little head," he said, moving so close he towered over her. "He's still breathing, and both of you can remain that way real easy."

Orville reached out and placed his hand against her cheek. She tried to flinch away, but his other hand gripped the other side of her head. He put on his best smile and lifted her in the air by her head until they were eye to eye.

"I'll let you in on a little secret," he mock whispered as his smile widened. "How easy it goes gonna depend wholly on your attitude."

The woman howled in fear as Orville carried her from the pond and flung her to the ground.

CHAPTER NINETEEN

Deputy Boyle looked up as the door opened. Pike stepped in with a nod and hung his hat on the rack near the front. There was a concerned look on his face as he moved toward the front desk.

"Sorry," Pike said with a grunt. "The drive to the motel took longer than expected. Why don't you go and grab some dinner and call it a night? I'll have Smite come in early to cover everything."

"Sure," Boyle replied as he stood. "Everything all right?"

"Honestly … I don't know," Pike said before turning and stalking to his office.

Boyle hovered a moment, unsure if he should follow. Shaking his head, he finally slipped out of the office and hustled across the street.

"Howdy, Deputy," Sarah, the waitress behind the counter, called out with a wide smile. "The usual?"

He nodded as he placed his hat on top of the table before sliding into the booth seat. Most people in town ignored him, but a few stopped by to say hello after they finished up their meals. Each wore a smile on their lips, but fear radiated from their eyes. Boyle tried to ignore it, focusing on anything pleasant he could come up with.

Soon, the diner was empty and Sarah appeared with a plate of eggs, bacon, and toast. He nodded his thanks as she set the plate down.

"Never met anyone who ate breakfast for every meal," she said, tapping her finger against her lips.

Boyle studied her finger, using it as an excuse to openly stare at her. She wore her long dark brown hair swirled into a messy bun, and he wondered what trick she used to keep it in place. Stray hairs popped out here and there, seemingly drawing attention to her every feature. Sarah's cheeks flushed red once she realized he was watching her.

"Not polite to stare," she said with a playful pout that made her green eyes sparkle.

"Apologies," he said, turning his attention to the plate in front of him, "but it's kind of hard not to."

Sarah laughed in surprise, her cheeks growing redder. "Why, you silver-tongued devil." She playfully slapped his shoulder when she walked by.

Boyle grinned as he began to scoop up the eggs. He ate quickly, like he'd learned in the Army. Sipping his coffee, he patiently waited for Sarah to return with his check. He enjoyed using this time to reflect, but today, he struggled to keep his thoughts in order. There was something hanging over this town, and he wasn't sure he wanted to know what.

"All done?"

He looked up from his coffee and nodded. *She's really quite lovely.* The thought took him by surprise, overwhelming him with a desire to extend their interaction. He struggled to come up with anything and blurted out, "Why is everyone afraid?"

Sarah froze as she reached for his plate. She stood still a moment, her eyes searching his face before issuing a sigh and slipping into the booth across from him.

"It's harvest season," she said in a way he expected she thought explained it all.

"Seems earlier than normal ... is that the worry, that the crops aren't truly ready?"

She stared at him a moment longer, then shaking her head, she said, "Has the sheriff not explained this to you? Not that you'd believe him. Deputy Smite's been here longer than most, and *he* didn't for the longest time."

"The sheriff? What does he have to do with the harvest?" Boyle asked, his confusion reflected on his face.

"Directly? Nothing," Sarah said, her finger back to tapping on her lips. She stayed quiet a moment longer, then moved to slide out of her seat. "It's too soon; you won't believe me."

Boyle reached out and snagged her wrist. He kept his grip loose so as not to hurt her. "Please, I want to understand."

Sarah glanced around before leaning close to whisper, "Best I can say is avoid the corn."

Boyle let her go, unsure what he was hearing. *Does she mean the corn growing across from the Tanners' motel?* He opened his mouth, but nothing came out, and Sarah gently pushed up on his chin.

"If the sheriff or Smite won't tell you ... maybe Ms. Westin can help."

Boyle studied her with unblinking eyes. He'd seen some stuff in the Army, but nothing that was so taboo no one would speak about it.

What have I gotten myself into? The thought settled heavy in his gut.

CHAPTER TWENTY

Smite stood in the baby's room, hovering over his son's crib. *Is the cost too great?* His chest ached at the thought. He reached down, resting his hand on the boy's torso. A mewing noise slipped from his son as the child's tiny hands wrapped around his fingers.

"Does it matter?" he whispered to himself.

No, not really.

In the background, the phone rang twice before cutting off. He stood still, enjoying the way his son seemed to be studying him. He was a special boy, a miracle, really.

"Ray?"

He stared at his boy for a few more seconds, cherishing the soft cooing. With a sigh, he pulled his hand away and turned to his wife. She stood in the doorway, already dressed for bed. He offered her a smile and stepped to her. His heart nearly broke as he studied the fear in her eyes.

"What's wrong?" he asked, reaching out and placing his hands on both sides of her upper arms.

"Sheriff just called," she whispered. "He wants you to come in early."

Pulling her in tight, Ray wrapped his arms around her and pressed his lips to her forehead. "Is that it, Ella? I bet Boyle just needed to leave. He's still getting acclimated to everything."

She buried her face in his shoulder as she trembled in his arms. He held her, enjoying her warmth of her pressed against him.

He pulled back, and when she glanced up, Ray leaned in and kissed her gently on the lips. At that moment, he knew whatever the cost, he would pay it.

✳✳✳

Orville stomped through the high grass, dragging the still unconscious man by his left leg. He wasn't too excited to try and carry him since the man was buck naked. *He'll be fine.* It wasn't like The Scarecrow cared how alive they might be when Orville left them. *At least not yet.* He shuddered at the thought.

"You better still be alive when we get there," he hollered over his shoulder.

The man moaned but otherwise stayed quiet. The sun would be setting soon, and the last thing Orville wanted was to be close to The

Scarecrow in the dark. He sped up, and the man issued another moan as he began to bounce more and more against the hard Texas dirt.

The corn was close; he could hear the wind moving through the stalks. The crows were issuing their cries, calling out as if to warn The Scarecrow that Orville approached. *That's silly.* A wave of fear filled his belly. *Is it?*

He spun around and pulled hard on the man's leg to jerk him into the air. Orville caught him, holding him tight against his chest before spinning back around and running as fast as he could. His breaths came out in ragged heaves, matching the crows as their caws filled the air. He glanced at the sky once more before sliding to a stop a few feet from the cornfield's edge.

Lifting the man above his head, Orville stepped forward and heaved him into the corn. The stalks bent down under the weight before springing back into place and hiding the man in the shadows.

"Gotcha another one, boss," Orville cried out.

The crows grew quiet, but the wind carried raspy laughter towards him. He didn't wait to see if The Scarecrow appeared. The laughter followed him as he ran away, only stopping when he passed the crosses.

CHAPTER TWENTY-ONE

Ruth stood in the middle of the cornfield. She stood on tiptoes, trying to see above the stalks but failing miserably. She was positive she heard a child's voice earlier, but now there was only the wind blowing through the corn. She glanced up to the sky, seeing how much longer until the darkness descended on the field. *Don't need Robert to remind me not to be out here once the sun's gone.* Although, she was pretty sure he'd be upset to find her out here any time of the day.

Her head shot to the left, 'he sound of giggles grabbing her attention.

"Anna?" she asked, her voice a whisper.

Ruth's breath caught as the giggles continued, gaining in volume. A crow's caw surprised her, and she stumbled back with a gasp. The bird landed where she'd just stood, studying her with its shiny black eyes. Her stomach twisted as her breath caught in fear. The crows terrified her, though she couldn't put her finger on why.

It hopped closer.'Ruth fought the urge to turn and run as the giggles grew louder. Her body trembled, but she willed her feet to take root. Another bird appeared, landing just behind the first. Slamming her eyes closed, she began to whisper the Lord's Prayer. The giggles retreated, and Ruth grew quiet. *Please, no ... come back.*

Slumping to her knees, Ruth buried her face into her hands and sobbed. *We are fools.* Anguish washed through her with each tear, and she wondered if it was possible for her to simply curl up and die out here in the corn.

"Momma?"

Ruth stilled. *It's not possible.*

"Momma, don't cry."

A slim hand rested on the back of her head. Trembling, Ruth peeked through her fingers. Her breath caught as she stared at dirty pale feet. Dropping her hands, her gaze traveled up until she was staring at her daughter's smiling face. Ruth sprang forward, wrapping her arms around the girl and squeezing her tightly. *Please be real.*

"Of course I'm real, Momma," she said with a breathless giggle.

Dry laughter filled Ruth's ears as she began to cry once more, struggling to ignore the sudden feeling of doubt overwhelming her.

Robert opened his eyes. He worked his tongue in his dry mouth, hoping to encourage moisture but getting a sticky mess instead. His stomach rolled, forcing bile up and burning his throat. He croaked out his wife's name but received only silence in response. Unsure where he found the strength, he swung his legs off the bed with a grunt.

After three deep breaths, Robert struggled to his feet. It was almost night, and his face burned with shame. *Why did Ruth let me sleep the whole day?* As he walked to the other room, a small burp slipped out, burning his mouth with an acidic taste. Outside, the crows began to cry. *What is going on?*

He froze at the thought.

The caws grew louder, making it hard for him to think clearly. Robert shambled into the room on unsteady feet. Pulling up, he stared at Nathan standing by the window.

"Nathan?" he asked, repeating the man's name with more force when he didn't turn.

"I'm sorry," the man whispered without moving.

"What did you do?" Robert asked, suddenly sober. He rushed over and gripped the man by the shoulder.

"I told her not to go out."

Robert followed the man's eyes and stared at the corn. The sky was dark with crows flying over the stalks, their cries building in volume until his ears ached. He wanted to pull Nathan away from the window and beat him until he explained what was going on, but instead, he continued to watch. *Oh, Ruth … why?*

The crows swirled upward, forming a tight tunnel, then exploding in all directions. Silence fell outside; the only sound now was Nathan's heavy breaths. Robert rushed outside, stopping at the roadside. A stiff breeze blew through the corn, shaking the stalks. A few crows landed on the other side of the road to study him.

His breath caught when Ruth stepped from the corn. She smiled at him, glancing down at the girl holding her hand.

Not any girl ... our girl.

Anna pulled away from her mother's grasp with a giggle and sprinted towards Robert. She wrapped her arms around his waist and gazed up at the stunned expression on his face.

"Why, Daddy," she said with a slight frown, "ain't ya happy to see me?"

Unable to speak, he offered her a nod while tears streamed down his cheeks. His Anna was back where she belonged.

CHAPTER TWENTY-TWO

Sam groaned. His body ached, and for a moment, he struggled to remember why. The last thing he recalled was kissing Jennifer in the pond … and then nothing. His eyes fluttered open. He stared at the hard-packed dirt and corn stalks. Confusion overwhelmed him, shutting down his thoughts.

"Where the hell am I?"

A tremendous racket sounded, drawing his attention to the largest gathering of crows he'd ever witnessed. With an explosion of movement, the tight grouping suddenly went their separate ways. A few landed on the ground near Sam. The biggest hopped closer until it was within reach. Its head turned back and forth, always keeping an eye on him.

What is it doing? Sam took a deep breath and struggled to stand. He covered his genitals with his hands, his face flush with embarrassment and worry. *At least no one is around to see.*

"Are you sure?" a raspy voice said behind him.

The crow cried out, startling Sam and making him jump. Trembling, he turned to glance at the speaker.

"I'm sorry, what ..." The question vanished, and he stared open-mouthed, trying to make sense of what he saw.

A scarecrow stood a few feet away, dressed completely in black, down to its gloved hands with tufts of straw poking out in places. A thick burlap skin covered the thing's head, with stitched lips and eyes made of the darkest, shiniest stone Sam ever saw. It held a short-handled scythe in its right hand.

It stood motionless, leaving Sam to wonder who just spoke. He stepped toward the scarecrow, and the crow issued another caw from behind him. He ignored the bird, fascinated by the detail put into the scarecrow and its attire.

Stunning how real it all looks.

The crow cried out once more, and he glanced back to see what might be bothering the bird.

"Really should pay attention to the main threat," the voice said, pulling Sam's attention back to the scarecrow.

The scythe slashed through the air, and the sharp blade sliced through his neck. His scream quickly became a gurgle as blood flooded into his throat. Sam teetered a moment, his fingers clawing at his neck in a vain effort to keep his head from sliding from the stump. The thin red line blossomed, spraying blood outward before Sam's head tipped from the smooth stump.

The Scarecrow laughed once again. Bending down, i' picked up the head and lifted it over its own. Blood dripped onto the burlap, slipping and sliding until it found the creature's lips. It tossed the head to the side, letting it roll away.

Sam wondered how he was seeing all this since his head was no longer attached to his body.

"That is only flesh," The Scarecrow said, pressing its hand against the corpse's torso.

Pain flooded Sam, blinding him momentarily. Once his vision returned, he found himself held tight in its free hand. Something was different, and after a moment, Sam realized he was not all there. He glanced back at his body, still lying in the dirt. Swinging his attention back to the hand clutching the front of his chest, Sam struggled to understand what he was witnessing.

There was a shimmer around his body, but it grew duller with each step The Scarecrow took. They entered a clearing; Sam couldn't be sure, but it seemed a perfect circle. He shook his head, surprised where his thoughts were wandering. At the center, The Scarecrow pulled back the scythe and slashed it through the air.

Sam attempted to blink away the sudden dazzling light that appeared. A jolt of tremendous weariness flooded him, and if not for The Scarecrow's hand holding him, Sam thought he might tumble to the dirt.

"I take no joy in this," The Scarecrow said, his attention completely on the slash.

The slash spun, a line of fire burning through everything. It grew and stretched until it formed a four by six square floating in the air. Sam leaned forward, searching into the darkness on the other side. More laughter slipped from The Scarecrow. It pulled Sam closer, stopping just before their skin could touch. The Scarecrow took a deep breath, drawing air through where its nose should be.

"Your fear and blood aroma is pleasing," The Scarecrow said, the thick stitched lips taking the appearance of a smile.

Sam struggled, but The Scarecrow's grip grew tighter.

"You're right to be afraid."

Tiny wordless noises issued from Sam, who now was locked onto the square hovering in the air before him. Black smoky tendrils slithered from the darkness and reached for Sam's dimming form. They wrapped around his wrists, sliding up his arms to meet at his neck. The shadow grew darker, spreading over Sam's body until he was himself a shadow.

"To add to the harvest is a blessing," The Scarecrow said in a quiet voice. "Best to hold onto that when it all begins."

"What are—?" Sam was cut short as The Scarecrow released him to allow the darkness to pull him through the square. Heat flashed through him, growing in intensity the farther he moved on the other side. A wordless howl issued from his throat, intertwining with the dry, raspy laughter he heard before. A chill ran down his back, but it only intensified the pain and terror and somehow amplified the heat coming from the other side.

The square began to shrink once Sam was through, the laughter coming from farther and farther away. The square soon was only a pinprick of light for Sam to obsess over.

"A blessing," The Scarecrow issued one final time before Sam plunged into complete darkness.

CHAPTER TWENTY-THREE

Smite walked into the office and sighed. Rumor was a bank over in Houston had something called centralized air, but he struggled to understand just how it worked. *Has to be better than open windows and some fans, right?* Maybe he'd get lucky and there'd be some activity around town.

"You don't mean that," Pike said as he exited his office.

"Sorry, sir," Smite replied with a nod," didn't realize I was speakin' out loud."

"If we're lucky, there won't be a peep," Pike continued as he stepped closer. "We got lucky today. Boyle reported all was well out at the motel. God knows how with the harvest startin'."

Smite nodded, unsure how to answer. It seemed obvious to him that the Tanners were there same as most everyone in this crazy town. Something was promised, and the price included building that motel. *Living here and looking the other way when necessary is the only way to survive.* Of course, didn't mean he thought them any less a fool living that close to the corn.

Pike slipped his hat on and sighed. "I'm heading home. You need anything, call."

Smite ran his pointer finger off the corner of his forehead in a half-assed salute. He sat down at the front desk to be closer to the breeze coming from the window and to have the phone within reaching distance. *All this getting up and down is for the birds.* He shuddered, suddenly thinking of the crows by the corn; crows that seemed to have a mind of their own.

"That's silly," he said out loud.

"What's silly?"

Smite shot out of the chair with a yelp and spun toward the window. His hand rested on his holster, but he didn't draw. He frowned at the woman standing there. "Jesus, Sarah, I could have shot you."

"Been my own fault, I reckon," she said with a snort.

"Did you have a reason to stop by, or was it just to eavesdrop?"

"Yes, but spookin' you took priority," she said, her smile growing wide. The silence stretched, and just when Smite was about to respond, she continued. "Deputy Boyle is asking questions. Thought you and the sheriff would be interested. The way he spoke tonight … well, I don't think he's seen The Pale Man."

Smite slowly nodded, he suspected the same thing. *No one comes to Donn without needing something unattainable.* He just hadn't figured out what Boyle was searching for.

195

"Okay, I'll tell the sheriff, and we'll take it from here," he said before motioning her to move along. "Now get."

"Thanks for the laugh, Deputy," she said between giggles, turning to walk back to the diner.

Smite waited until she crossed the street and then sat down. Maybe tomorrow they'd find out what brought Boyle to town. *There's always a reason.*

Orville stomped back to his shack, a chicken under one arm and a yellow dress he snatched from his neighbor's place in his other hand. He wondered how long the man lasted once he entered the corn. *From the sound of those crows, not very.* He smiled, knowing The Scarecrow would be content with his offerings. At the very least, he would have plenty of time to explore his newest plaything.

The sun was dropping, and with that, the temperature. The shack was unbearable during the day. Not that he ever stayed in there long enough for it to be an issue. His daddy worked in the mines back east when he was a boy and developed a need for the underground that Orville almost immediately picked up.

Once he was on his land, he glanced around, searching for any signs of trespassing. *Don't need any nosy deputies poking around right now.* Convinced he was alone, he hurried to the shack. He took a deep breath, opened the door, and rushed to the bed in the back corner. His face turned red, a combination of holding his breath and the heat captured in the room.

Orville let the chicken go and reached under the bed. His hand found the heavy padlock about halfway to the wall. He flopped to his belly, slithering under the high frame. It was a bit of a tight squeeze now, but his father had been a large man, so it was manageable. Popping the key into the padlock, he unlocked it and pulled it free.

A blast of cold air met him as he swung the trapdoor just enough to slither into the opening. Using his feet to lower the trapdoor, Orville crawled a ways, only stopping when his fingers brushed the lantern. He struck a match and lit the wick, wincing when the fire worked its way to his fingers. A soft glow filled the tunnel, and he began to crawl.

The tunnel widened out and eventually grew to an enormous oval chamber. Orville stood, stopping every few feet to light the few candles he kept down here. Those mixed with sunlight sneaking in through the number of shafts his daddy dug for ventilation lit the chamber enough he was able to put out his lantern. The smell reminded him of all the days his daddy left him underground.

Those days were terrifying, trapped with just enough oil to last a few hours and having to decide when to use the light. For the first few years, he burned it until it ran dry, plunging him into darkness. It wasn't until he was older and more comfortable in the dark that he started to conserve the oil for emergencies.

Orville stepped to the far wall and looked down. The light made its way a few feet before being swallowed by the dark. A soft whimper rose from the depths. He squatted and smiled. *Might take less than normal to break this one.* He stood and stepped to a spike hammered into the wall of packed earth.

He hung the dress there, enjoying the clean scent wafting from it. His hand hovered near the fabric, but he pulled away after a moment. *Wait for the right moment.* He smiled at the thought as he flopped down on the makeshift mattress across the room. *Plenty of time before the harvest ends.*

CHAPTER TWENTY-FOUR

Pike stood in the middle of the corn. Shaking his head, he struggled to remember why he was out here. The sun was just dipping below the horizon, plunging the field into darkness. His heart pounded against his chest. *Figure it out when you're home.* He started to run through the stalks as the crows began to cry out. A dry, raspy laugh followed him through the corn, pushing him to speed up.

A pinprick of light shone brightly up ahead, doubling in size with each step he took towards it. The laughter grew in volume, drowning out all other sounds, until his ears ached from it. He was getting closer to the light, and a sudden swell of relief filled his chest.

I'm close—

A jolt of pain across his throat cut the thought short.

Pike's hands clutched at his neck as he slid to a stop. The pain built as the laughter continued. His eyes widened as The Scarecrow stepped from the shadows, holding up his scythe. The blade was dull from blood. *His blood.* His heart dropped at the thought. Scrambling to hold it together, his head began to tip backward.

The darkness swirled around as his head tumbled to the hard-packed earth. The Scarecrow stepped closer, leaning down to grip the sheriff by his hair. The light in the distance disappeared as he came eye to eye with The Scarecrow. Pike's mouth opened and closed like a fish out of water, but nothing came out.

"If the harvest continues to be this insufficient," it whispered, "there will be consequences."

The Scarecrow swung its arm high, releasing Pike's head to fly through the air. A screech filled his ears as a large crow raced toward him.

Pike woke with a jolt. His wife shifted, reminding him she was asleep in the crook of his arm. He stared at the ceiling while struggling to bring his breathing back under control.

She barely weighs a thing. The thought tugged at his heart. There was a time he'd complained her sleeping like that left his arm numb. *Those days are long gone.* He cherished every second they shared now, knowing the doctors believed she should have died all those years ago. The cancer had eaten through her like those termites in his old shed. As long as they stayed in Donn, he was able to extend their time together.

A bang from the other end of the house grabbed his attention. He gently shifted Doris and slipped from their bed. She groaned slightly at the inconvenience but stayed asleep. Pike grabbed his revolver and stepped lightly into the hallway. He moved through the house, stopping to check each door on his way.

"There is no need for a gun," a voice said as Pike stared toward the kitchen. His heart pounded as he pushed the door to enter.

He swallowed hard when his eyes met with The Pale Man's. He sat at their kitchen table, two glasses already filled with whiskey in the middle. He nodded to the open seat, which Pike took after a moment's hesitation. *I'm not awake.* The gun disappeared from his hand with a burst of smoke as if to emphasize his thought.

"Are you unhappy with our agreement?" The Pale Man asked as he selected one of the glasses.

"No-o-o," Pike stammered, glancing back the way he came.

"Are you sure?"

Pike nodded, his gaze still focused on his bedroom.

"Then why are you failing to keep up your end of the bargain?"

The Pale Man slammed his hand against the table, startling Pike and bringing his attention back to the table. Even with cheeks flush with anger, The Pale Man practically glowed white. Pike blinked, unsure what to say.

"It's only been a little over two weeks," he finally decided on. He ignored it best he could, sending the two deputies to check up on the motel. Every time they returned, there was no change. *Well, except that second time.* Pike was still surprised the Tanners brought a child to the area.

"Leaving you with less than a week to meet the quota," The Pale Man said, snapping off at the end of each word. "You have squandered two-thirds of the time agreed upon. Did your predecessor's fate teach you nothing?"

Pike stopped breathing. He stared at The Pale Man. They had found his predecessor nude and hanging from the church's rafters two years ago Sunday. The word *DECEIVER* carved into his chest. Pike was sure the man had done it with his own fingernails. That death promoted him to sheriff, and with that, a new pact. *Meet the quota or the cancer returns.*

"Forgive me," Pike said, struggling to take enough breath to answer. "There is still time, and you will receive the agreed-upon amount."

The Pale Man smiled, flashing his razor-sharp teeth. "See that you do."

Pike's eyes shot open, a dull ache in his chest. He struggled to rise from the bed and lurched to the bathroom. In the mirror, he studied the backward letters carved into his chest. *DELIVER.*

CHAPTER TWENTY-FIVE

Ruth Tanner stood at the edge of the road. She stared at The Scarecrow standing on its perch as the sun rose. There was a pleasant breeze moving through the corn, and she shuddered when it pressed against her nightgown. The last few days had been scorchers, and she wondered if they shouldn't head over to the pond Nathan was always going on about. *It sounds li'e something a normal family would do.*

Glancing back at the motel, she frowned.

After nineteen days, Ruth suspected they were anything but normal. She was wrong to pressure Robert to come here, wrong to accept the deal. Swallowing, she returned her attention to The Scarecrow. *Too late for regrets, I guess.*

"Mom?"

She bit her bottom lip, wrapping her arms around her chest. The voice was spot on and filled Ruth's heart with joy. Yet there was something else there, something just under the surface that terrified her. Her insides squirmed in discomfort as she turned from the corn.

Anna stood in the doorway, rubbing at the sleep in her eyes. When they lost her, she was fourteen and just beginning to show signs of her approaching womanhood. Ruth remembered how excited she was when she discovered her girl was growing up. When she found her in the field, Ruth realized while Anna was the same age, her body was even more developed than before. Her daughter's breasts were fuller, rounder, and required Ruth to alter one of her bras to fit the girl.

The morning light shined through Anna's nightgown as she stepped toward her mother, the illumination only accentuating her curvy figure within the nondescript fabric. Her breath caught as her daughter flung her arms around her and buried her face in her bosom. The girl burned hot, and within a moment, a slick sheen of sweat covered Ruth.

She fought the urge to push her daughter away, instead wrapping her in a light hug. The high temperature had worried her at first, but now that almost three weeks were behind them, she understood the child simply ran hotter than before. It didn't make sense, but Ruth understood none of it did, so she stopped trying to question it all.

Easier said than done. Her stomach rolled at the thought.

Another breeze came from the corn, bringing with it cool relief. Sighing, Ruth buried her face in her daughter's hair, struggling to ignore the dry, raspy laughter that came with the wind.

✳ ✳ ✳

Orville lay on his mattress listening to the gentle snores coming from the hole. It took a few days, but exhaustion finally overtook the woman. *She's been sleeping like clockwork ever since.* He simply blew out the nearest candles, and she took that to mean night. In a few minutes, he'd light them back up, and by the time he was ready to lower some breakfast, she'd be wide awake.

Soon she'll be beggin' to come up … to help me … to serve me. His lips curled into a wicked smile. From that point on, he could do anything he wanted to her. Standing, he shuffled through the cavern until all the candles burned. He lowered a chunk of bread and the end of a cheese rind in the small basket he used for anyone in the hole.

Orville stretched and moved to the table in the center of the chamber. He sat in the chair closest to the hole, pulled out a hunk of wood, and began to whittle, a trick he picked up from his daddy on some of their longer spells waiting for trouble to pass.

"Hello?" the woman called out, her voice unsure.

Orville stayed quiet, his heart beginning to beat faster.

"Please … are you there?"

He stood, making sure to push the chair back so it made a sound. He walked to the hole and knelt to peer over the edge. Mostly, all he saw was darkness, but as she stood, her face shone and her wide eyes reflected the dim light. She was prettier than most he caught out here, almost exotic with her short blonde hair and pale skin. He wished there was more light so her body was easier to see, but deep down, he knew the wait would add to his excitement.

Not like you didn't get an eyeful at the pond. He nodded to himself, knowing he'd looked but in the end, refused to touch. It took all Orville had not to mount her at the pond, but something stopped him, something made him think it would be better if she gave herself to him. So, he'd studied her laying on the grass, trying to hide her naughty bits. He stifled a groan as the memory of her nude body excited him, then forced the memories away; wouldn't do to ruin the moment now by not paying attention.

He focused on her face, enjoying how it slipped in and out of the Shadow down in the hole.

"Thank you," she said, holding up the bread and cheese and offering a toothy smile. "It's so good."

"Mrs. Potter makes a fine loaf," he said, returning her smile with one of his own. He made sure to keep it simple and tried to reflect the joy in his eyes. He was well aware of how some of his smiles affected the women in town.

"Is that … your wife?"

"No," Orville answered, surprised she said wife instead of mother like most women asked. "I don't have a wife."

"Oh … so no one to … care for you?" she asked in a hushed tone.

"No."

"Did I hear a chicken?" she asked just before the silence dragged out too far.

Orville blinked at the sudden change in topic.

"Yes."

"I fry a mighty fine chicken if you got the fixin's. Do you like fried chicken?"

Orville sat back, moving away from the hole so his smile could widen. *Right on schedule, and better yet, she was suggestin'.* He trembled with anticipation, struggling to catch his breath enough to speak.

"Yes, ma'am. I surely do, but I need to get some things done before I dispatch the bird. More importantly, so do you."

Orville pulled back, grabbing a hook pole and three buckets. He lowered them, each time waiting for her to reach up and take the bucket. A sigh of relief came from the darkness. His smile widened.

"I know how appearance is important to you gals," he said in a rush of excitement. "You got some fresh water, some towels, and in that third bucket ... I found you a pretty dress and some ribbons for your hair, if you are so inclined."

"Thank you again ..." she trailed off before coming back with a question. "What's your name? I'm Jennifer, but call me Jen."

He mouthed her name, trying it out but not giving it voice just yet. Walking back to the ladder, he listened to her breathing before replying. "My name is Orville, ma'am. I'll go get busy while you pretty yourself up."

The only reply was the splash of water.

CHAPTER TWENTY-SIX

Boyle glanced in the passenger-side mirror of the station's only prisoner transport, a converted Model T Stake Bed. Smite was behind the wheel, driving as if they didn't just pick up six men from a neighboring stationhouse. All six men wore chains, and no paperwork exchanged hands. He found that mighty suspicious. Then again, he found pretty much everything in Donn a bit off.

"What are we doing?" he asked, expecting to get stonewalled once again from Smite.

"Our job," Smite answered, letting the silence build in the cab for a few moments before continuing. "Why are you here? Not in the truck but here ... in Donn?"

Boyle glanced at him from the side, the question taking him a bit by surprise. The few months he'd been around Smite, he'd never come across as direct. "I found out there was an opening here, and I needed a job."

Smite pursed his lips, appearing to be mulling over the answer before sighing. "That's it? Nothing else compelled you to come here specifically?"

Does Smite know? Worse yet, does Sheriff Pike? Boyle stared out the passenger side window. He was in Donn because Barry Miller wanted him here at Ma's behest. Boyle knew it would have been career suicide to refuse Ma's wishes. *You don't say no to the political machine in power.* So he moved to the middle of nowhere and started to watch.

"I just wanted some peace and quiet after getting out of the service," he finally answered. "They said Donn was quiet."

"Most of the time," Smite said under his breath.

Boyle ignored him, knowing full well there wouldn't be a clear explanation. His thoughts wandered back to his talk with Ms. Westin earlier in the week. She'd offered nothing. In fact, after hearing his answer to a question similar to the one Smite just asked, she'd clammed up.

Boyle glanced at Smite. *Is there some special reason he is in Donn?* Maybe he was going about it all wrong. He nodded slowly to himself, returning his attention forward. *Maybe there's a reason everyone winds up in Donn.* He'd start with Sarah at the restaurant to test his theory.

Pike stood in the lobby of the Tanners' motel. He absentmindedly scratched at his chest as he smiled at the young woman standing behind the counter. Something about her unnerved him. She stared at him with unblinking eyes a moment before disappearing into the back. She returned with Robert in tow and motioned to the sheriff.

"Ah, Sheriff," Robert said as he moved to shake his hand. "What brings you out?"

Glancing at the girl a second, he turned his attention back to Robert and sighed. "The boys are transporting some prisoners for a neighboring town. We need to let them stay here overnight before moving on. We'll pay, of course."

Robert nodded. His stomach rolled with unease, and his chest tightened. He wasn't sure having criminals so close to Anna was a good idea. He said as much to the sheriff.

"This is your daughter?" Pike asked, his gaze shifting to the girl when Robert motioned towards her.

The young lady stepped from behind the counter and slid next to Robert. Pike tried not to stare but something about the girl pulled at his attention. She was tall for her age, which he had been told was around fourteen. Everything about her seemed more mature, and he wondered if he might have the age wrong.

Her skin, while pale, held a healthy, ruddy glow just beneath the surface and paired well with her dirty blonde hair, which hung just past her shoulders. But it was her dark brown eyes that affected him the most. *She has the eyes of a predator.* His insides turned to ice when she smiled at him and extended her hand.

His 211hrough211on to take her hand only seemed to enhance her satisfaction because her smile widened. His stare rested on her teeth, and he winced when the tip of her tongue snaked out and slid over them. His eyes moved up to hers, and their gazes locked as he took her hand. His breath caught as the image of her naked body squirming beneath him flashed through his head. Pike jerked his hand away and stepped back with a shudder.

"You okay?" she asked with a knowing wink.

He nodded slowly, forcing himself to focus on Robert's face. The man simply shrugged.

What the hell is going on here?

"I'll have at least one deputy here the whole time," he mumbled before stepping so close their belt buckles were touching. "This isn't up to me. You've stayed alive this long for a reason … I'm sure *he'll* keep you safe."

Robert stepped back, wrapping his arm around the girl's shoulder. He nodded. "Okay … so later today, you say?"

"I imagine you have a few hours before they arrive. Smite is in charge."

"Will do, Sheriff," Robert said to Pike's retreating back.

A blast of heat met Pike, and the bell jingled as the door closed behind him. The ball of ice in his belly melted, making his insides feel loose. Spitting to the side, he stared at The Scarecrow across the street. *Who thought something worse might arrive one day?* He spun around when the jingle sounded once more.

"Been a while, huh?" the young woman asked with knowing eyes shining.

Pike swallowed hard, trying to ignore how the thought of touching her made him stiffen. She stepped closer, her bare feet practically hissing on the hot asphalt. Her arm rose up, her hand pressing against the word carved into his chest; the rough fabric of his shirt making the wound itch. He looked down, his eyes locked on her deep red lips as she spoke with a voice husky with desire.

"You do what needs to be done, and I'll make sure you get a … just reward." Her hand slid down his chest and rested on his belt buckle.

Trembling, Pike reached down and pulled her hand away. He tipped the bill of his cap, cleared his throat, and began to step backward toward the cruiser.

Something much worse.

CHAPTER TWENTY-SEVEN

Fred stood on the edge of the cornfield opposite the motel. *Wouldn't do to have the Tanners see me.* He assumed they owned the corn with the way Earl talked, but since they weren't working the field, he figured he'd help himself to a bit. Earl and Nathan were acting all strange when they were putting the finishing touches on the motel, but all he could think of was making hooch.

Just mentioning the field made those two seize up like a couple of ninnies. *Best to just provide the drink, then have to listen to their nonsense.*

This was his third trip to gather corn. The first batch was a little weak, but the second one would be done today and should be perfect. *Just in time to share with the boys.*

Fred jumped, dropping all the corn on the ground when a crow cawed loudly behind him. Grumbling, he picked up a corncob and spun around, flinging it at the bird. The crow hopped to the side, easily dodging the projectile. It studied Fred a moment, then cried out once more. A number of replies came from within the field.

Fred began to scramble across the ground, scooping up the corncobs. A sudden breeze stirred the stalks, carrying soft, raspy laughter to his ears. The crow hopped to the corncob closest to it and picked up the corn with its beak. It held it out, head cocked to the side as if waiting for Fred to take it.

Fred glanced around before reaching out a trembling hand to grasp the end of the corncob. The bird opened its beak and let loose a burst of caws, then sprang into the sky. Standing, he followed the crow with his eyes as it circled lazily above the cornfield, unease settling over him. Fred swallowed. He wouldn't admit it out loud, but he was pretty sure the bird was mimicking the laughter on the breeze.

Ruth stepped next to her husband and stared out the window.

"I was thinking of taking Anna to the pond Nathan was talking about," Ruth said as she tried to ignore how close the girl now stood next to the sheriff. She sighed in relief when the sheriff backed away to his cruiser.

"Sure … if you think it'll be okay," he said after a moment.

He's getting slower each day. Like his mind is growing fuzzy. Ruth's attention swung to the door as their daughter walked in. She wore a crooked smile that made Ruth flush red in embarrassment. She could only imagine what was running through the girl's mind. *Nothing good, that's for sure.*

"Your momma's gonna take you to the pond. Be a good idea to cool off on such a hot day," Robert said in that lazy way he now spoke every time Anna was near.

Anna slid closer, her bottom lip sticking out just a little. "But not you?"

Robert shook his head with a sigh. "No, honey. Maybe next time. We actually have guests coming soon."

Ruth reached out her hand towards her daughter. "How about we get out of Daddy's hair?"

A look of disappointment flashed over Anna's face but was quickly replaced with that crooked smile as she took the offered hand. Ruth led her from the room, fighting the urge to pull away from the girl. Her skin crawled while her chest grew tight with trepidation. Although she wanted the girl away from her husband, Ruth realized she wasn't too keen to be alone with her either.

"I'm just so happy to be here, Momma," Anna said, releasing her mother's hand to twirl around the room.

Ruth stood quietly, desperately wishing she felt the same.

CHAPTER TWENTY-EIGHT

Orville stood in the pond, the water up to his waist and a bar of soap in his hand. He didn't much remember his momma, but he recalled her fondness of a well-washed man. So before every interaction with a new guest, he made sure to visit the pond. Although, in truth, he did this because he enjoyed the lingering smell of the woman on his skin once the fun began.

Chattering floated to the pond on a blast of hot summer wind. He pulled back, slipping his large form into the tall grass at the edge of the shore. He slipped as low as the water would allow, hiding most of his frame under the water's surface. His eyes widened as the lady from the motel appeared across the way with a younger girl in tow. *What did the deputy call her ... Mrs. Tanner?* The woman was apprehensive, and Orville was pretty sure the girl was the reason.

He studied the young lady, desire building deep in his belly. At first glance, she was a younger version of Mrs. Tanner, with long slender limbs, long blond hair, and the same wide lips. She let loose a laugh as she slipped her loose-fitting shirt over her head before wiggling out of her shorts. His eyes slipped down her body, taking in her developing breasts, curvy hips, and bare legs.

"Momma, this suit you made me is just so beautiful," she said, her voice low and gritty.

Pressure began to build in his groin as she extended her arms and began to spin slowly to show off the suit to her mother. Orville's eyes widened as everything seemed to stop around them save the girl. His breath caught as the girl's skin darkened to a golden honey hue while chestnut highlights darkened her blonde hair. She seemed to grow as she spun; her torso lengthening, adding emphasis to her curves as her breasts and ass swelled in size. She stopped suddenly, facing the tall grass he hid within.

Orville refused to blink as the girl brought her arms in, resting her hands over her enlarged breasts. With a crooked smile, she ran her hands down her stomach, stopping with her fingers pressing against her crotch. Biting her bottom lip, she began to rub and massage the area. Trembling, tiny breaths of excitement slipped between her pursed lips. He shuddered when her nipples grew hard and pressed against her swimsuit.

Blood filled Orville's mouth as he bit down hard to suppress a moan while waves of desire washed over him. She winked in his direction and jumped into the water. He jerked forward, time no longer moving slower than normal. When the girl broke through the surface, she was back to normal.

Orville blinked. *What just happened?*

She swam back towards her mother, who now sat on the edge with her legs in the water.

"Careful," Mrs. Tanner said, kicking her legs back and forth. "You never know what might be in the water."

The girl laughed, glancing at the tall grass. "Nothin' I can't handle."

CHAPTER TWENTY-NINE

Jen squatted over the bucket, trying to ignore the sound of her stream striking the side. She grabbed the washcloth from the newest bucket she'd received from Orville before he left. Wringing out the water, she wiped her privates with eyes closed and savored the coolness against her skin.

Where is he? Not that she was eager to find out how it would all play out, but Jen was ready to leave the hole. He had every chance to violate her at the pond and in the cavern, but he didn't. She hoped to play off that. At least until a chance at escape presented itself. She dropped the washcloth back into the bucket and stepped to the rest of the items her captor had lowered in the hole.

Smiling, she held up the dress. It was nothing special, just a simple yellow cotton house dress, but her eyes welled up with tears as she pressed the material to her face. *When did I last wear clothes?* Jen desperately wanted to put it on but hesitated, terrified it might get dirty down in the hole. Biting her lower lip, she pulled it over her head, sighing as the soft fabric slid over her skin.

She grabbed the hem and pulled it up as she bent over to picked up a hairbrush. Even in the shadows, she could tell it was beautiful, something precious to the man who held her captive. Running it through her hair, she shuddered as the bristles swept across her skin. She hoped he got back soon, afraid the longer she stayed down in the hole, the greater the chance of a misfortune occurring.

"Sheriff?"

Pike looked up from the paper to find the town librarian staring at him. He folded it closed and nodded to the booth seat across from him. She raised her hand towards Sarah before sitting down.

"What can I do for you, Ms. Westin?" he asked between sips of coffee.

"Now, Sheriff, how many times do I have to tell you to call me Abby?"

"That's a losing battle, hon," Sarah said, pouring coffee in Abby's cup, then motioning towards the sheriff. "Top you off?"

"Please and thank you … Ms. Carter."

Abby's eyes gazed up in exaggerated exasperation as she poured sugar into the dark brew. She stirred her coffee, seemingly waiting for

Sarah to finish. Pike took a sip, wincing at the heat on his lips as he listened to the steady ting from her stirring.

"Deputy Boyle may be an issue," she finally said after blowing on her coffee. "I don't think he is here same as the rest of us."

"Ya don't say," he said, waiting for more. Deputy Smite already informed him of the talk he had with Ms. Carter a week ago.

"This is no joking matter," she snapped, her jaw quivering a bit. "Someone in Austin is curious, curious enough to send a man to investigate."

Pike nodded slightly. "True. Someone is curious … Deputy Boyle."

Shaking her head, Ms. Westin reached across the table and grabbed his hand. "Damn it, Charles. He doesn't know The Pale Man."

Pike glanced at her hand before moving his attention back to her face. "I understand your worry, but what's done is done."

Ms. Westin pulled back, wrapping her hands around her cup. They sat in a silence broken only with the occasional sip. Pike fought the urge to pick the paper back up and instead simply stared at the town librarian. Pike understood what he had to lose if outsiders came in, but he avoided the reasons why many of the town's folk chose to be in Donn. *Not important, and not my business.*

"Ma'am … Abby," he said, leaning closer to keep his voice low. "I'm not worried about Austin. Leave my deputy to me, and by the end of the harvest, all will be as it always has. I have no doubt."

She nodded, offering a slight smile, and stood. "Thank you, Sheriff," she managed to say before bursting into tears and hurrying from the diner.

DONN, TX 1926

We all have crosses to bear here in Donn, Pike thought before reopening his paper.

CHAPTER THIRTY

Robert stood on the side of the road facing the corn, his eyes locked on The Scarecrow. Five crows perched on the cross beam. The stalks swayed slightly as a gentle breeze came from the north. Sweat ran down his brow, into his eyes, but he didn't blink. His insides turned to water as he forced his first step onto the road. The crows began to cry out, but whether in encouragement or warning, he couldn't tell.

He needed to know the truth about The Scarecrow. He needed to know if his family was in real danger or if it was all his imagination. He let Deputy Boyle blow him off all those weeks ago. *Someone did die out in the corn.* Robert just needed to find the evidence to show them. *Is that all?*

The crows grew louder as his feet stepped down onto the side of cornfield. There was no mistaking their intent now with each cry getting more and more aggressive. Guttural laughter came from the corn. A lump formed in his throat, his chest tightened, and he struggled to breathe.

Do you really need to do this?

The question repeated in his mind, blurring the words together until all he heard was a low roar warning him not to continue. A crow landed in between him and the corn, issuing a caw that made Robert take a step back.

"What do you want, Robert?" a voice asked from the corn. It was low and raspy, like the laughter.

He glanced between the stalks and the corn until the question repeated.

"What do I want?" he whispered. He chewed on his bottom lip, unsure what to say.

More crows landed until there were ten of the birds between him and the corn.

"Yes, Robert?" the voice responded with a sigh. "What do you want? Or is it need?"

The largest crow hopped closer, its beak opened wide. He eyed the bird, afraid if he moved, the thing would attack. The others issued subdued cries to each other, seemingly ignoring the man before them. Robert trembled as waves of terror built in his chest and washed outwards throughout his limbs.

His tongue, heavy and thick in his mouth, lay still as the crow advanced. Robert swallowed hard and blurted out, "My family to be safe."

Laughter built within the corn, suddenly drowning out everything in Robert's world. The crows all squawked before taking to the sky to circle above the field.

"Ah, Robert," the voice responded once the crows grew quiet. "The threat to your family does not reside in the corn."

Robert's mouth hung open, but nothing came out. There was a ring of truth in the voice, one that made his stomach drop. For if the voice could be trusted, then the threat to his family was already in the motel. Which only left him a handful of choices, choices he didn't think he had the strength to face.

"Mr. Tanner?"

Robert turned slowly to find Nathan standing in the parking lot, a concerned look on his face.

"Yes, Nathan?"

"The rooms are ready … You all right?"

"Yes, of course," he replied, stepping away from the corn. "Everything's Jake."

Orville finished lighting the candles before stepping to the edge of the hole. Jen's eyes shined with hope, and he offered a smile while holding up a finger. He stepped away and grabbed the makeshift ladder he kept nearby. She released a whoosh of breath when he reappeared to lower the ladder into the hole. She waited to touch it until he motioned for her to come up.

Ain't this the bee's knees.

Jen climbed to the top, and Orville held out his hand to help her finish her ascension. She stood with her hands clasped in front of her and her head down. The dress was a tad too large in the chest and hips, but it was close enough. Her hair shone from all the brushing, and he stepped closer, slipping his finger under her chin to tip her head back.

She offered a shy smile, offset by the panic shining in her eyes. Orville stiffened. *Too soon.* By his estimate, there were at least a few days before the harvest ended. He wanted to enjoy her company, to have some home cooking before enjoying her other pleasures. *Maybe she's the one.* He smiled at the thought. No matter, it was a win-win situation for him.

"Do you like …" she trailed off, her hands now grasping the dress as she swayed slightly, her eyes still downcast.

"You look lovely," he said, remembering hearing someone say the same to the pretty waitress in town.

Jen's smile widened, to his delight. This was going better than any of his previous guests.

"What's in the bag?"

He glanced to where she pointed, then stepped over to the table, reached into the paper sack, and pulled out an apple. Her eyes widened, but she didn't move. Orville walked over to her and held it out, nodding when she continued to stay still. Jen reached out with a trembling hand and wrapped her fingers around the smooth skin of the fruit.

Orville fought the urge to sigh as her fingers slid against his hand a moment. Her touch was electric. He stared at her, enjoying how her lips parted as she moved the apple to her mouth. He winced at the loud crunch of her teeth cutting through the fruit. The juice ran from the corners of her lips as she chewed. Orville stiffened as he watched her devour the apple.

He'd give her a choice: be his forever or meet The Scarecrow.

CHAPTER THIRTY-ONE

Smite pulled the truck into the motel parking lot. Sheriff Pike leaned against his cruiser.

"You know he was coming?" Boyle asked as they came to a stop.

"Nope. Sure he has his reasons." Cutting off the ignition, Smite stepped from the truck and raised his hand in greeting. "Howdy, Sheriff, everything all right?"

Pike stood straight and nodded. Gravel crunched under his feet as he stepped closer to the prisoner transport. The other door slammed shut, and Boyle slid next to Smite. Pike stopped a few feet away, tipping his brim toward the men.

"Any trouble?" he asked after a brief pause.

"No, sir," Boyle said as Smite shook his head in answer.

"Good. I've made a deal with Tanner, and we're going to keep the men here until the exchange can be made."

"Sir?" Boyle said, stepping forward to close the gap. "Is that wise?"

"Huntsville has a bus coming through in a day and wanted to grab these men on its way back," Pike said, turning his head to spit. "They prefer not parading through town to pick up some goons when they can just stop out here. That okay with you?"

Boyle offered a terse nod, keeping his eyes on the ground.

Smite sighed and stepped forward to pass Boyle. *When is this man going to learn?*

The lobby door opened, and Robert Tanner stepped out with a large key chain. He shuffled to the three men, stopping a few steps behind the sheriff.

"Mr. Tanner here is giving us the largest room in the middle. It's been cleared of anything loose and only has the front-facing mini window and the larger window facing out back," Pike said, pointing to the door marked with a golden number three.

Tanner stepped toward the room while Smite spun on his heel and hoofed back to the truck. He started it up and backed it closer to the room's door. Boyle and Pike marched over to the tail of the truck, waiting for Smite to return with the keys. The truck's engine cut off, and Smite hurried to the back, handing the keys over to the sheriff.

"You men and I are going to come to an understanding, real quick," Pike announced as he stepped up into the back of the truck. He glared at each man in the stifling shadows before holding up the keys. "I will unlock you, and then you will go through that open door, where, if you behave, you will be fed and allowed to rest until Huntsville arrives. If you give me an ounce of attitude, I will leave you in this sweatbox to die. Do I make myself clear?"

All six men stayed quiet but nodded with no hesitancy. Pike unlocked the first man and, after he stepped down, moved to the next. Smite and Boyle helped each man lower down from the back of the truck, the shackles making it cumbersome. A line formed until all six men stood single-file between the two deputies.

Pike hopped down and clapped his hands loudly. "Let's get inside, boys."

Boyle led them inside the stripped-down room. Smite brought up the rear as the sheriff walked back to his cruiser. The men shuffled to the middle, where two rows of three chairs sat facing each other. Boyle gestured to the chairs, and each man sat down with a sigh. Two large fans blew from each corner, and though the room was still hot, at least the air was moving.

The sheriff entered with two bags and set them on the table in the corner. He pulled out two thermoses, and Smite recognized the aroma of the diner's coffee after he unscrewed the top of one.

"Our local diner was gracious enough to make you goons some sandwiches and coffee. Of course, it's hot as the devil today, so I brought some of their lemonade as well. Mr. Tanner, do you by chance have any ice?"

Tanner poked his head through the doorway and nodded. He held out the door key, which Smite took. *What a weird man.* A moment later, Smite remembered there was a Mrs. Tanner and she was most likely uncomfortable housing six criminals. Smite helped Boyle pass out the sandwiches wrapped in wax paper. Each man took the food with a nod but none began to eat.

Tanner returned with a bowl filled with ice chips and nine cups stacked together. He placed them on the table and quickly left the room. Smite made six drinks and motioned to Boyle to help him pass them out.

Pike produced sandwiches for his deputies but only drank some of the cool lemonade. Boyle and Smite refrained from both, their eyes locked on the six men in the middle. Once the prisoners finally ate, Smite motioned to Boyle to eat while he continued to keep watch over the prisoners.

"Smite, you have everything under control?" Pike asked as he moved to the door. After Smite gave a nod, he continued. "Boyle, with me for a moment."

Smite swung his attention back to the men in the room, his hand sliding to his holster. *So it begins.*

CHAPTER THIRTY-TWO

Nathan stepped back from the window. A blast of nervous energy shot through him as he walked back to the table.

"Fuzz's here," he said as he sat down.

"So? Mr. Tanner told you they were coming," Fred said with a snort. "Ain't no reason for them to come over here."

Nathan glanced at the case of hooch sitting over to the side. *No reason they know about it.* Sheriff Pike seemed pretty loose with the rules in Donn, but Nathan never met a lawman who didn't want a taste of the product or profit. *Most likely both.*

Earl shook his head. "You ain't got to worry about Pike. He's well in hand."

Nathan waited for clarification, but Earl just sampled more from the Mason jar in front of him.

"What did I tell ya?" Fred said with a grin. "Stuff is mighty smooth."

Earl nodded and took another drink. Nathan sipped the clear liquid, wincing at the burn as it traveled down to his stomach. They all decided Nathan's was the best place to store the excess since he didn't have the stomach for the stuff. Plus, they hoped the motel would draw more potential customers.

Smacking his lips, Fred brought his jar up and drank deep. Nathan stared with wide eyes. *How is he doing that?* Earl smiled and poured a little more into his jar before screwing on the top. He offered each man at the table a salute and drank as deep as Fred. Nathan set his jar down, for the most part untouched, and stepped back to the window.

He studied Mr. Tanner carrying some glasses and a bowl toward the room where the sheriff was keeping the men. *What's he got there?* A moment later, he reappeared empty-handed and practically ran back to the lobby. Nathan wondered just how long Mr. Tanner would survive out here. Especially since their daughter had appeared out of nowhere.

Nowhere?

Nathan shuddered at his unconscious effort to wash the truth away. She came from the corn somehow, walked out holding her mother's hand like they were leaving Sunday Service.

"Now what?" Earl growled from the table. "You want to get the sheriff's attention, keep staring out that window."

Nathan glanced back, noting his jar was now resting between Earl's cupped hands. "Not the sheriff ... just Mr. Tanner. Well, now Pike's out with the new deputy. Maybe take it easier on that stuff."

"Maybe go fuck yourself," Earl growled, his voice brimming with anger.

Nathan's cheeks darkened, his chest burning with fury. He stared at Earl as he finished off the shine in his glass and moved to get more.

"Y'all know what ... we need a woman," Fred blurted out. "Maybe we should go find the missus. Would love a taste of that." He punctuated the thought with a burp.

"You think she's something special, you should see their daughter," Nathan said, the words suddenly thick on his tongue.

The image of the girl filled his head, but not the girl who exited the corn. No, the image he pictured now was clearly a woman. But even that fell short; she was all things sensual, a carnal manifestation. His stomach burned, but he wasn't sure if it was the shine or desire creeping up from his groin.

"A daughter?" Earl asked, slurring the words. "How old?"

Nathan stared daggers across the table, frowning. He slapped his palm against the tabletop. "Old enough ... but she's mine."

Earl leaned back, his eyes flashing in anger. Fred reached over, placing his hand on Nathan's shoulder to stop himself from falling out of his chair.

"Of course," he whispered with a gentle squeeze, "but friends share."

"Not this," Nathan whispered through a clenched jaw. "Not her."

"Why the fuck not?" Earl roared as he sprang from his seat, shoving the table aside. "Don't even think about hoggin' that pussy."

Nathan stood straight, his eyes locked on Earl. His vision burned, a red hue cloaking over everything. His jaw clenched so tight it ached, and his hands balled into trembling fists. And yet, he could tell his friend was even angrier. His entire frame shook as spittle flew past his twitching lips. Nathan glanced at the crates once more.

"Where did you get the corn?"

Fred stood on unsteady legs. He swayed a moment, a sick grin on his lips. "Who am I to pass up free corn?"

"Oh, Jesus …"

CHAPTER THIRTY-THREE

Pike stared at his newest deputy as they stood in the middle of the parking lot. The silence built between the men until he was sure he could reach out and grab it. *Use it to beat this mother fucker into submission if necessary.* He hoped it wouldn't come to that. It never had before, but like his daddy used to say, *there's a first time for everything.*

"Deputy Boyle, this is your first season, so I'm trying to cut you some slack. In fact, I'm going to do your job for you. Take the cruiser back to the office. I'll stay with Smite."

Boyle clenched his jaw as his hands balled into fists. Pike shifted his weight in anticipation, but the man didn't move forward. They locked eyes a moment, and Pike understood the truth. Boyle wasn't one of them. He didn't belong in Donn.

"Hey, Sheriff," a woman called out. "Everything all right?"

Pike waited until Boyle looked away before searching for the owner's voice. His chest tightened as his eyes fell on Anna before realizing it was her mother who spoke. Both ladies wore towels, their wet hair hanging in tangles. His eyes tried to focus on Ruth, but they darted back to Anna.

She clenched her towel tightly, displaying a figure he wouldn't have thought possible on a girl her age. Her breasts strained against the fabric, threatening to pop free with a simple deep breath. His stomach dropped at the thought. A seductive smile danced across her lips, and he returned his attention to her mother.

"Why yes, Mrs. Tanner," he said as he tipped the brim of his hat towards them. "All's well, but I'd suggest getting inside. You don't want these men seeing y'all … especially like this."

Ruth's cheeks colored slightly, and he wondered if his words sent her thoughts to the Peeping Tom from their first night. She nodded before reaching out to grab Anna by the arm and guide her through the lobby door.

Boyle continued to watch them until the door closed. He swung his attention back to Pike with a sigh. "Anything else, sir?"

Pike shook his head and held out the keys to the cruiser, which Boyle snatched as he stomped off. *At least the man still follows orders.*

The steering wheel creaked as Boyle gripped it. He took a deep breath, forcing his jaw to unclench. *Something is going on. Something important.* Nothing added up, but he had nothing to go on except his gut, the same gut that got him through the war. Boyle learned years ago to trust that feeling when it showed up deep in his belly.

He pounded his fist against the wheel as he sped away from the motel. He was well aware the reason they sent him to this godforsaken town was whatever was going to happen behind him. The car passed the pond he assumed Mrs. Tanner and her daughter returned from. *If they hadn't shown up when they did …*

He l't the thought trail off. *What would I have done?* Boyle shook his head. *Doesn't matter now.* He glanced up through the windshield as a dark cloud blotted out the sun. The sky above was an ocean of black with tiny beams of sunlight trickling through. A roar of concentrated noise washed over him as the darkness began to pulsate.

Boyle struggled to pull his eyes away from the mass as he barreled down the road. He didn't expect anyone to be out here, but he knew it was better to have his eyes on the road ahead. Black streaks shot from the darkness. *Are those crows?* His throat tightened at the thought. *There're so many.*

They struck the vehicle, slamming into the metal with a sickening crunch. More and more continued to strike the cruiser, bouncing off the vehicle to be crunched under tires. The glass cracked and splintered until the birds began to slide through. Boyle cried out in shock as the crows opened and closed their beaks, issuing loud cries of pain and frustration. The beaks clacked together, the sound reminding him of his time watching the Flamenco dancers at the end of the war.

His foot slammed on the brakes. The birds struggled to push through the windshield; a few slipped in through the open side window. He howled in pain as their razor-sharp beaks sliced into his exposed skin. The wheel slipped from his grasp as he flailed around, slapping at the crows to drive them away. The car spun off the road with a screech and entered the cornfield.

Boyle's head struck the steering wheel when the car slammed to a stop. His vision faded as he stared past the writhing birds at the giant cross set at the edge of the cornfield.

CHAPTER THIRTY-FOUR

Orville carried a chair to the stovetop set up at the end of one of the offshoot tunnels. His pa designed it so any smoke was sucked up and out of their home. He wondered how it worked but had given up trying to understand it when his constant questions irritated his pa. Once he crossed a certain line, he knew a beating was coming. Best to stop before you even sniffed the line.

Jen stood in front of the cast iron stove top with her hands on her hips. Orville's tongue ran slowly over his lips as he stared at her backside. He hadn't told her yet that there was a chance she could be spared. He wouldn't admit it, but deep down, he was scared. Scared she'd choose The Scarecrow. What if he was that revolting? His pa always said it was so.

Instead, Orville simply sat and watched her scoop big globs of lard from the can and drop them in the heavy cast iron pan. The chicken rested off to the side on a small table that was close enough to the oven to offer a workspace. Plucked clean and butchered, the chicken simply needed to be breaded and fried. He'd left everything she would need in a bag on the table.

He already fed the heat box with charcoal, and the tunnel was growing warmer. It would be worth it once his teeth sank into that fried chicken. Until then, he would enjoy the view. The dress was already sticking to the backs of her legs just above her knees. He liked the way her calves looked in the flickering light. A clearing throat grabbed his attention away from her legs.

Jen was looking over her shoulder, an eyebrow raised. Orville felt his cheeks grow hot while his belly squirmed. She turned to face him, crossing her arms just under her breasts. He chanced a glance, enjoying how she now pushed them up a bit more. His gaze lingered a bit longer than he planned, and she cleared her throat again.

"And does the naughty boy see something he likes?" she asked, her voice husky.

Orville's eyes widened, unsure what to say. His heart pounded against his chest. None of the others ever spoke to him. They might plead or beg but never *talk*. Jen stepped toward him, the hem of her dress riding up a bit with each step. She swept her hand through her hair, slipping it behind her ear. Orville stared at her bare neck as she stopped a foot away.

The firelight reflected in her eyes as she studied him. His throat tightened, unsure what to say or do. He shifted in the chair, growing more uncomfortable by the second as his erection strained against the denim of his overalls.

"Oh, you poor thing," she cooed, bending at the waist to give him a direct view down the top of her dress. He strained to see her breasts within the shadows, but it was too dark. Her hands rested on his knees, and she offered a squeeze. "I see all this excitement is getting to you."

Orville followed her gaze to his crotch. A soft groan slipped out as her hands moved to the front flap on his overalls. Her fingers struggled with the buttons for a brief moment before slipping into the opening. He gasped as her fingers, still slick from the lard, gripped his erection and pulled him free.

Jen locked eyes with him, biting her bottom lip, her hand slowly moving up and down. He quivered, gripping the sides of the chair as she built up speed. His breaths came in quick gasps that matched her rhythm until he released with an exaggerated grunt.

Jen pressed his flaccid penis back through the opening and wiped her hand on his overalls. "There. Now go get cleaned up so we can enjoy this fried chicken."

Orville sat slack-jawed, his eyes following her as she moved back to the stove. He staggered to his feet, pushing the chair off to the side, and stepped to his pile of clothes across the chamber. He dug through the pile looking for a cleaner pair. A smile bloomed on his face as he thought about what might occur after they ate.

CHAPTER THIRTY-FIVE

Robert studied Anna as she stared out the front window. Ruth was in the back, washing up, he imagined. *She never was one to like pond water.* Didn't seem to bother his daughter, but then again, they were both bone dry by the time they returned. She glanced back, flashing a smile before returning her attention to whatever was outside.

The girl's growing up before my eyes … literally. She'd only been here for a handful of weeks, but his little girl was anything but all of the sudden.

"Daddy," Anna called out, her voice caressing the word. "Somethin's going on."

Robert pushed up from the counter, grabbing the bat he kept up front since the night of the peeper. He wanted something close at hand to brain the next fool that came by. Of course, if the issue was with those six the sheriff brought, he'd have to let it be. As long as they stayed away from his family, he couldn't imagine any reason he'd need to use it.

He walked up behind A'na, stopping to leave a'few inches between them. He peered over her shoulder, looking through the gap in the curtains. Across the way, a row of crows was standing on the other side of the road. He counted fifteen in the main row, but more of the birds landed and made their way to the line.

Anna reached to grab Robert's free hand and pulled his arm around her waist. She moved back, grinding her ass against his crotch as she wrapped her arms over his. She leaned her head back, resting it in the nook of his left shoulder to not block his view. Robert focused on the birds, attempting to ignore the heat radiating from the girl. A sigh of contentment slipped from her lips.

"I wonder what they are up to?" he whispered as they began to march across the road. He could only assume they were still lined up once they hit the asphalt because they were now out of his line of sight.

He wanted to move to the side window to see, but instead, he simply held onto the girl. His mind reeled as the scents of the pond filled his nostrils. Except he knew deep down it wasn't the pond that was holding him captive. It was something else, something he couldn't place. A mixture of scents that reminded him of so many things: the first time he met Ruth, the time they made love in the tall grass, the day his daughter was born, his favorite meal, and so much more.

Robert burrowed his nose into Anna's hair and breathed deep. His chest tightened and his stomach dropped while waves of emotion washed over him. He grew hard, partially from the sensations and partially from the pressure from her ass as she continued to press back.

"Robert?"

His eyes shot open, suddenly aware his hand was cupping Anna's full breast.

Jesus Christ, what am I doing?

He stumbled back, grateful the shock of his wife's voice had killed his erection. Anna spun around with an exaggerated pout before focusing on her mother in the far doorway. Robert couldn't be sure, but he thought he saw a flash of anger in her eyes.

"Momma," she said in that sing-song way she seemed to use more and more lately. "Those crows are actin' awfully funny."

Ruth stepped into the room, ignoring Robert completely, and continued over to her daughter. Robert hovered behind the two women, close enough to see but not intrude.

"See," Anna said as she pointed through the side window.

The crows were now lined across the parking lot, cutting the asphalt off from the road. Anna reached over and took her mother's hand. Ruth grew rigid for a moment, then relaxed.

Robert lost count after forty-five as more of the birds appeared from the sky to land just on the border of the motel. He offered a glance toward his wife, the thought of laying his hand on her shoulder crossing his mind. Instead, he gave a sharp shake of his head and rushed from the room.

Nathan swung his head between the other two men. They stood spaced out evenly in the center of the room. He noted Fred's legs pressed against the bed, but Earl was unhindered. He was also closest to the door. Nathan needed to figure out the best way to navigate them away from his escape.

Why escape? Kill these two, bathe in their blood, and then take the girl. Nathan's eyes widened at the thoughts in his head. His hands clenched into fists as he struggled to stop himself from springing towards either man. He blinked, hoping to clear his vision, but the red hue only seemed to deepen.

"You assholes think you can trick me?" Fred grumbled, his lips twisted into a snarl. His fingers flexed around the neck of one of his bottles of hooch, And the clear liquid sloshed inside as he waved it about.

"No one is trying to do anything," Nathan said, forcing each word out before they morphed into the ones screaming in his head. *I WILL FUCKIN' KILL Y'ALL!*

"Speak for yourself," Earl growled, holding up a switchblade base in his right hand. His other hand hovered in front of him, fingers spread wide. "Of course I'm trying to trick y'all. I've been doing it for so long, why stop now?"

Rage flashed through Nathan, the red hue intensifying until all he could see were blobs. His jaw creaked as he clenched it, his teeth grinding in his ears. He needed to leave or he was going to kill these men. His legs tensed, ready to propel him past his supposed friends and to the door.

Earl's eyes shifted to study Nathan for a moment before returning his attention to Fred and his bottle.

I must not be a big enough threat unarmed.

"That's right," Nathan cried out, channeling his rage into the words. "Earl was telling me how he was going to take all your shine and leave you with nothin'."

"Is that right?" Fred said, pulling back his arm before slinging it forward and releasing the bottle.

Nathan didn't wait to see if it struck true or not, instead sprinting towards the door. The familiar twang sound of the blade releasing from the hilt filled Nathan's ears as his hand grasped the doorknob. A bottle shattered against the wall, and a blast of pain struck Nathan in the middle of his back. He pulled the door open enough to slip out and stumble into the parking lot.

He spun in a circle, reaching with both arms to where the pain was sharpest. His fingers grasped nothing but his shirt as he struggled to find the knife. Harsh laughter came from behind, soon washed away by the cries of the crows standing by the road.

Fred and Earl both held bottles now. Before they advanced, Earl smashed his against the wall. Nathan slipped to his knees, struggling to find his breath. The crows continued to screech, cheering on the men as they neared their prey. Nathan moved to scream for help, but only black ooze ran out as it filled his mouth and throat. He choked on the thick sludge.

Earl gripped his hair and jerked his head back to expose his neck. Nathan struggled to swallow, hoping to force the blockage down. Insane giggles slipped from Fred as he moved his bottle from hand to hand. His eyes, large and shiny with excitement, focused on Earl, who pressed the bottle's broken edge against Nathan's skin. The jagged glass tore across his throat, flooding his senses with pain.

His hands flew to the wound, trying to stop the bleeding. Fred howled in excitement as he hopped around the two men, while Earl continued to dig the glass into Nathan's face and neck.

The red hue slipped from Nathan's vision as a strange calm washed over his body.

"I'll give you something to smile about," Earl growled, driving the jagged edge into Nathan's left eye with a loud squelch.

Pain bloomed in the socket, and he could feel the man twisting and turning the shard in the hole. Before he could offer more than a whimper, Earl stabbed the glass into his other eye.

Lost in darkness, Nathan howled, fear replacing the calm he just had. The back of his head exploded as Fred drove his unbroken bottle against his skull over and over until it split open, exposing his brains to the hot Texas air. The crows drowned out his cries as they moved closer to the men. Nathan hoped death came quickly.

CHAPTER THIRTY-SIX

Pike leaned with his back against the door. The prisoners were all finished with their meals and talking quietly among themselves. Smite stood across the room by the bathroom. He fidgeted with the nightstick handle sticking up from his belt loop.

Keep those heebie-jeebies under wraps. Pike stared unblinking at his deputy, hoping the thought got to him.

The prisoner closest to Pike lowered his head and closed his eyes. A moment later, gentle snores issued from the man. Smite grew still as he studied the remaining men.

Pike shifted his weight to stand straight. *Wouldn't do to not be ready if one of these animals rears up.* If they caught on before passing out, they could have their hands full.

The second man followed suit, soon followed by three, four, and five.

"What da hell y'all do?" the last prisoner asked, glancing back and forth between the two lawmen.

"Why, nothing at all," Pike said with a grin. "Your friends are just tired after a long day."

Smite nodded his agreement, stepping closer to the prisoners. The man's eyes narrowed as he studied the sheriff. With lips pursed, he began to say the word they all were thinking, *bullshit.*

A series of screeching cries from outside pulled Pike's attention away from the man. He motioned to Smite to keep an eye on the prisoner before spinning around and opening the door to investigate.

"Jesus Christ," he called out, sprinting outside and leaving the door open.

Pike couldn't tear his eyes away from the mayhem of the parking lot. He sensed Smite pull up behind him to peer over his shoulder. A wall of black slid closer as a jumble of crows pushed towards three men. Pike was pretty sure it was the usual suspects of Earl, Nathan, and Fred, but something wasn't right. They were thick as thieves at the worst of times, but when he saw Earl drive what looked to be a broken bottle into Nathan's face, he guessed something had changed.

The noise from the crows drowned out the screams from the men as they continued to struggle with each other. Fred hopped around, waving his arms, then he slammed the bottle he held into the back of Nathan's skull. Pike drew his firearm as he marched toward the three men. Smite was breathing loud enough to let him know the deputy was following.

"God damn it, Fred," he called out, struggling to be heard over the birds' racket. "Drop the bottle ... now!"

Fred grinned at the sheriff and held up his arms.

Pike eyed the bottle held tight in the man's grip. "I said drop it!"

Giggles slipped from Fred as Earl slinked up next to him. He held something tight in his grip, but Pike couldn't make it out.

"Knife ... I think," Smite called out as he pulled away from the sheriff.

"Now listen, you two—," Pike was cut short as Fred shot forward, swinging the bottle over his head. He let the man advance four steps before pulling the trigger.

Fred staggered when the first shot stopped his momentum. The next two sent him backward. Pike stood calmly, waiting to see if another shot was required. The birds' cries rose to a crescendo, drowning out all sounds save their own. Smite hurried to intercept Earl as he moved closer to the sheriff.

Fred swayed slightly, and Pike wondered what was holding the man up. A sharp cry pulled Pike's attention over to his deputy, who was struggling with Earl. A red stain bloomed on his shirt near his shoulder. Earl leaned closer, his jaws snapping as he tried to get any of Smite's flesh into his mouth.

"Fuck ... get him off," Smite cried, panic overtaking his usually calm demeanor.

Pike lined the sight with the back of Earl's head and squeezed the trigger. The crows took to the sky as the report echoed all around the motel. The sheriff's stomach lurched as he focused on the large hole where Earl's skull should be. Brains and black muck slopped from the wound, plopping to the asphalt below. Blood oozed down to soak into the man's shirt.

Smite bent at the waist and emptied his stomach of its final contents.

"Y'all fuckin' murdered him," prisoner six cried out as he shuffled from the room.

Pike noted the man's struggle to walk and guessed they just didn't use enough to knock him out. *Oh well, doesn't really matter as long as he dies.*

CHAPTER THIRTY-SEVEN

Ruth stood frozen, staring out the window. Anna knelt in front of her mother, her chin resting on the window, the sill gripped between her fingers. At first, Ruth wanted to shoo the girl away, but as the action unfolded on the other side of the glass, she found unexpected comfort from the girl's presence. She wrapped her arms around herself as the men from Nathan's room struggled in the parking lot.

"Robert?" she said so softly she wasn't sure if she actually spoke. Her bottom lip quivered as she struggled to call once again for her husband.

Ruth trembled when she saw the sheriff and his deputy appear and approach the men. Her gaze shifted to the right, drawn by the motion of the birds advancing. Three shots rang out. Anna leaned back and clapped in excitement.

"Look at the man dance, Momma," she said with a giggle, pointing towards Fred as he swayed around before tumbling to the ground.

A blur of motion drew their attention back to the struggle. Ruth reached down, laying her hand on Anna's shoulder before leaning closer. Earl and the deputy struggled. Smite cried out, and Ruth saw a knife stuck in his shoulder. The sheriff calmly raised his revolver once more and aimed at Earl. Her breath caught as she waited for him to pull the trigger.

Ruth jumped at the loud report, sending her daughter into another giggling fit. She pulled her hand away, moving it to cover her mouth, eyes wide in shock. A prisoner shuffled by the window, moving towards the corn with constant glances back to see if the sheriff moved to stop him.

"Why is he letting him just go?" she wondered aloud.

"Don't worry, Momma … he won't get far," Anna said.

Smite gritted his teeth as he gripped the handle of the knife sticking in his shoulder. Pike holstered his weapon and stepped over Earl to take a closer look.

"Don't," he said, spitting off to the side. "Best to have the doc give it a look. Let's get you in the lobby and see if we can't get word out."

Smite offered a terse nod and let go of the knife.

A series of screeches pulled the men's attention up to a dark cloud of crows swooping towards them. Smite threw up his hands to protect his face as the birds rained down. Pike let out a startled curse before disappearing for a moment in the feathered mass.

The birds gathered the three corpses from the ground and carried them over the road into the corn.

"Jesus," Smite hissed, turning to gauge the sheriff's reaction.

"Huh," Pike said, spitting once more to the side. "Wonder if they'll help with those sleeping beauties in the room?"

As the two men stepped to the lobby, the sound of an unexpected laugh brought a grimace to Smite's lips. He locked gazes with the Tanners' daughter and shivered at the glee reflected in her eyes. *No one should be forced to see all this violence, let alone a young girl.* Yet he expected this girl chose to watch what just happened, and that chilled him to the core.

CHAPTER THIRTY-EIGHT

"Keep movin', Kevin," prisoner six said out loud in encouragement. *Why ain't the sheriff givin' chase?* He glanced back one last time to witness the cops disappear in a sea of crows. *No reason to look a gift horse in the mouth.* He smiled at the thought and slipped into the stalks.

Now if only there was a way to get free of these bracelets. He stared at the handcuffs as he pushed through the corn. If he kept moving, maybe he'd stumble across a farmhouse. For now, he was just pleased to be away from the madness at the motel.

The cries of the crows grew louder, sending a blast of adrenaline into Kevin. *Whatever they slipped us is wearin' off.*

He stumbled into a small clearing, tumbling to his knees. On the ground was a rusty old hand scythe. A smile split his face as he scrambled to snatch it up. *This may work.* He ran the blade against the inside of the left handcuff, struggling with the angle. A loud caw sounded from above, and he glanced up to find a crow perched on a scarecrow's shoulder. The scythe slipped from his fingers.

Kevin scrambled back, kicking up dust. *Is that thing watchin' me?*

Dry laughter followed him as he attempted to regain his footing.

"Where are you going, offering?" The Scarecrow asked, stepping from its perch.

It scooped up the discarded scythe and pointed it at Kevin. "The season draws to a close, but be proud with the knowledge your soul adds to a fruitful harvest."

A wide shadow appeared above, plunging Kevin and The Scarecrow into the shade. A whimper slipped past Kevin's lips as the thing advanced. A glint shone in the deep black circles The Scarecrow wore as eyes. Three bodies fell to the ground with sickening thuds, then the shadow above dispersed as the crows issued more caws and flew apart. A streak of sunlight shined on the extended hand of The Scarecrow. It filled Kevin's vision until all he saw was the rusty blade.

Hot urine spread out from Kevin's crotch as the creature gripped his hair and pulled him to kneel before it. It pooled around his knees before soaking into the dust. He trembled in anticipation as The Scarecrow pulled the scythe back.

"This is just the beginning."

Its voice reminded Kevin of crunching dry leaves in his hands as a child. *Oh God … I'm so sorry.* His thought never made it to his lips. The scythe slashed down, cutting through his neck in one clean slice.

The Scarecrow caught the head as it tumbled from Kevin's shoulders. Holding it over its burlap face, the creature let the blood drip over its thick brown lips.

A large crow flew over to perch on its master's shoulder. The bird pushed its beak between the burlap and the steady drip of Kevin's blood. After taking its fill, it issued one final caw and hopped down to land on one of the three discarded bodies.

"Yes … yes, all in good time," The Scarecrow said.

The Scarecrow slashed the scythe, forming an opening in the air. It tossed Kevin's head into the darkness. Turning, it grabbed the first body and lifted it. The creature sighed, gazing at the blood-soaked man in its grip. It tossed the body through the rent, followed up with the other two corpses, then finally ripped the diminishing spirit from Kevin's chest. It carried the writhing essence to the opening and pushed it through. The Scarecrow waved the scythe over the tear, sealing the darkness away. A large group of the crows descended, landing on Kevin's body until all that could be seen was a black shivering mass.

CHAPTER THIRTY-NINE

Jen glanced back to study the room one final time. She offered a shy smile when she realized Orville was watching her. Her stomach rolled as the thought of his naked body pressed upon her flashed through her head. *If you don't get out of here …*

She let the thought go unfinished. She realized how lucky she was so far, since Orville seemed to be acting out some bizarre fantasy. But Jen understood the fantasy would turn at some point, and not in a way she wanted. No, what she wanted was to find Sam and keep heading south. A lump formed in her throat at the thought of her fiancé. The last time she saw him, Orville was handling him like a ragdoll.

Her eyes locked onto the tunnel entrance that sloped up and out of sight in the back corner. If she could get past Orville, Jen was confident she could get to the tunnel. Then her fate would depend on luck. *But you have to try.* She nodded at the thought and returned her attention to the melted lard.

Jen grabbed the metal coffee cup left on the table. She dragged it through the hot fat and placed it back down. She then tossed in the first few pieces of breaded chicken.

Taking a deep breath, she shuddered and called out, "Orville, sugar, did you want anything else with this chicken?"

Her eyes closed as she waited. The sound of the chicken frying was the only sound for a few moments. *Please.* His chair creaked, sounding as if it might break any moment, and Jen opened her eyes. She reached over, looping her fingers in the handle of the cup. She winced as the hot metal burned her skin and bit her bottom lip to keep from crying out.

Turning her head a fraction, she caught Orville approaching her. *Careful,* she warned herself, knowing moving too soon would be the end of her attempt at escape. He cleared his throat.

"Naw, just the chicken, then dessert."

Jen's eyes widened. *He's close … closer than I expected.* He moved with a light step, and she wondered if it was too late to act. She fought the urge to jerk away when his hand lay on her shoulder, the heavy weight reinforcing just how much larger he was than her. Her heart pounded in her chest. She forced her free hand to reach up and rest it on his. *Now or never.* The thought gave her the strength to move.

She gripped his fingers, pulling his hand from her shoulder, and spun to face him. As she turned, she flung the cup towards his face. Orville stood frozen in confusion, his eyes darting between her and the hot lard flying from the cup. She released his hand and sprang forward, attempting to slide by.

Jen made herself smaller as she scraped against the rough dirt wall. A roar of pain ripped from Orville as his hand went to his face and he stumbled back, tripping over his feet. She dove forward, past the entrance to the main cavern, landing with a grunt. Quickly, she rolled to the right just as Orville tumbled to the ground, groaning in pain. His hands stayed pressed against the red angry skin of his face. Jen lurched to her feet and ran towards the back exit. His howls of anguish followed her as she entered the tunnel.

"You gonna die for this, bitch."

Jen tried to block out his cries, but they followed her down the tunnel, each time promising her pain and death. Tears ran down her cheeks as she fought to catch her breath. The tunnel grew smaller, forcing her to her knees and then to crawl. *How did that man ever make it through this?*

The tunnel grew dark as she left the candlelight behind, and she wondered if she made a mistake. *Did I choose the wrong one? Is there another way out?* Jen's chest tightened at the thought. Another roar came from below, followed by the sound of breaking furniture. *Oh God, he's up.* She thought there would be more time to escape.

"You are going to fuckin' die!" he yelled over the snapping wood. "The Scarecrow will dine on your scraps."

Jen sobbed, not understanding the actual words but comprehending his meaning. A gasp slipped out as her hands struck wood just above her head. She pressed, struggling to move it until she stood. Light shone through a crack, growing in size as she continued to push.

"DEAD ... you hear me?"

She scrambled through the opening, hissing when the wood scraped down her calf as she pulled herself from under a bed. Standing, she shuffled to the door, ignoring the mess all around her, the call of freedom stopping her from taking a moment to rethink her plan.

Jen gripped the doorknob as the bed exploded upward, slamming into the ceiling before crashing off to the side. Orville struggled to pull his bulk through the trapdoor opening. She stared at his face, frozen by the grotesque way the lard had disfigured his skin. She thought of a thick candle burned to the base, the wax droopy and running over the edge of the holder. Orville's face looked like this now, showing sections of bone and muscle that leaked bloody mucus from the openings.

"You did this," he wailed, crawling toward her. "Now I'm gonna introduce ya to the devil."

Jen snapped back and turned the knob to slip from the building. She stumbled down the stairs, her ankle twisting and giving out on the bottom step. Sprawling onto the hard mix of dirt and gravel, Jen struggled to regain her breath. She crawled over the jagged rocks, ignoring the pain from the number of cuts forming on her bare skin. Struggling to her feet, Jen let out a sigh of relief. There was a building just a ways from the bottom of the hill. Even if it was empty, she was pretty sure she could hide in the cornfield just past the road.

CHAPTER FORTY

"Mr. Tanner … Robert, a little help," Pike called out as he held the door open for Smite.

Ruth rushed forward, reaching toward the knife, but stopped short and instead ushered him to sit down. She hurried to the back rooms. Anna slinked forward, stopping a few feet away before dropping to sit cross-legged on the floor. She leaned forward, resting her chin on her palms. Pike glanced at the girl, his eyes sliding from her face to the opening caused by her hanging shirt.

Damn it man, focus. He tore his gaze away just as Robert entered. His face was drawn, his mouth turned down into a frown, but it was the dullness of his eyes that made Pike shudder. *Maybe he finally understands what he signed on for, what he sold his soul for.*

"Do you have a phone?" he barked, pointing at his deputy. "We need to get the doctor out here to help Smite."

Robert studied the blood-soaked shirt and the knife handle protruding from the deputy's shoulder. Sighing, he nodded and stepped over to the counter. He reached over and pulled up the phone. Robert pulled the earpiece up to his ear and held the phone close enough to talk directly into the mouthpiece.

"Hello? I need Doctor Crawford up at the motel. Deputy Smite has been injured."

He replaced the earpiece on the hook and placed the phone back on the counter. Ruth appeared with a pitcher of water and some towels. She pressed a damp towel just below the knife wound. Anna rose to her feet and moved closer.

"Can I help, Momma?" she asked with wide eyes.

Ruth motioned for her to take over holding the towel. The blood soaked into the white weave, turning it pink. Anna glanced back with a gleeful smile. Pike noted the difference between her eyes and her father's, and it frightened him. *Something isn't right with that girl.*

"Doctor should be here soon," Robert said, making no move to step any closer.

Pike patted Smite on his uninjured shoulder and tipped his brim toward Ruth. "Thank you, ma'am. Robert, you're gonna need to come with me."

Pike stepped outside, and Robert joined him a moment later. The two men stood in silence, staring up at the black swirling mass of crows as they flew above the cornfield. Their caws filled the air. He turned his attention to The Scarecrow's perch, his expectation rewarded when he found it empty.

"We don't really have any time for delay," Pike said loud enough to be heard over the crows. "I'm not sure just how far The Scarecrow can reach, even with the crosses gone."

"Far enough, I reckin'," Robert mumbled as a hush fell over the motel and cornfield.

The two men rushed to room number three. They entered the room, and Pike pointed to the closest man sleeping on the floor. Robert and Pike knelt down and grabbed the man to carry him from the room. Pike shifted his arms, slipping them to hold the man by his armpits while Robert struggled to hold the man's legs.

They shuffled as quickly as the weight allowed until they stood on the opposite side of the road.

"On three," Pike said as they began to swing the man back and forth.

They released their hold when Pike called out the number, and the man flew towards the corn. He struck the ground with a thud and rolled into the stalks. A trio of large crows landed in front of Pike. He stared at the birds, aware they were watching both of them.

"You tell that bastard we got four more coming," he growled, resisting the urge to draw and fire on the birds.

A hot breeze rustled through the corn, bringing dry raspy laughter to the men. "Will it be enough, Sheriff, or will I get to visit your lovely town once again?"

"You know the deal," Pike shouted to the disembodied voice. "We still have time to meet your master's quota."

More laughter was the only reply, and the men turned to move the next body.

CHAPTER FORTY-ONE

Boyle groaned and opened his eyes slowly, wincing at the setting sun's light glaring through the shattered windshield. He swiped his hand across his forehead, pulling it away to display a smear of blood. *Explains the pain.* His eyes focused on the windshield, looking through the filtered sunlight to find a number of crow carcasses trapped within.

He wondered what made them do that, attack his vehicle. In the end, he realized it didn't matter, and he opened the door and slid out. *As long as they leave me be now, it will be all right.* Using his arm to rest his weight on the car, Boyle took a few deep breaths. He wasn't too far from the motel. Better chance of getting help there than hoping a car actually drove by. He was well aware that most people avoided this road. Taking one last breath, he pushed off of the car and shuffled forward. After a few feet, he felt his strength returning, and his pace increased.

Shading his eyes from the sun, Boyle stared at the black mass forming in the distance. He assumed it marked where he would find the motel. When they sent him to Donn, they told him something strange was going on. *They have no clue.* He shook his head. *Do I?* Nothing he' dug up made any sense, and no one shared enough to give him more than the most distorted of pictures.

Boyle knew he had a choice to make once he got back to town. He wondered if he would make the right decision. *Is there a correct one at all?* A chill ran through him at the thought. His view on the world always came to things being black or white, but whatever was going on here didn't fall into either … at least not on the surface.

A loud cry overhead pulled his attention upward. A number of crows flew by to join the growing flock. He moved to a trot, hoping to get there in time to see what was causing such a commotion. His head pounded with each step, but he ignored it as best he could. *There'll be plenty of time for headaches after this is over.*

The door closed with a bang, and Orville stalked towards it, shuffling through the garbage strewn about. He saw everything through a red haze as the pain in his face pulsed with each step. He fought the urge to reach up and touch the damage and instead focused on what he planned to do to the woman.

"I would have given her everything," he growled, his throat tightening at the betrayal.

His gaze fell upon a shard of broken mirror uncovered by Jen's escape. Orville sank to his knees and snatched up the piece to stare at his reflection. *Where are my lips?* His eyes burned as tears welled up. He wanted to blink them away, but he couldn't stop staring at the horror gazing back at him. *Can they fix this?*

Sobbing, Orville flung the mirror against the wall with a crash. When he was little, his daddy always said that deep down he was a monster. *Ain't deep down anymore.* Leaning forward, he rested his hands on the floor as he suffered through a series of dry heaves. The rough scratch of burlap against his hand grabbed his attention. He lifted the discarded sack and studied it a moment, then ripped two holes in the material.

Orville slipped the burlap over his head and stood. Maybe it was for the best. He opened the door and stepped from his house. He could see Jen moving towards the motel and the cornfield. It was time to introduce her to the monster she set free, and then he would gift whatever was left to The Scarecrow.

CHAPTER FORTY-TWO

Jen was halfway to the cornfield when she noticed Orville on the top of the hill. Her stomach rolled, and her mouth filled with saliva. She was walking as fast as her twisted ankle would allow, but she knew it wasn't fast enough. Grinding her teeth, she forced herself to speed up. She saw the large gathering of crows disperse, with many disappearing into the stalks.

She hoped someone was available to help her at the building. *Not sure I can keep this up too much longer.* Worst case, she would try and disappear in the corn. She prayed it didn't come to that. Her eyes brightened as she got closer and saw the sign proclaiming the building was a motel.

"Thank God," Jen mumbled, a burst of adrenaline allowing her to speed up once more.

She refused to look back when a scream of rage came from the hilltop. She feared just the sight of him advancing would drain her last bit of resolve. Her throat tightened, and tears streamed down her cheeks. She was so close.

"Please," she called out as she approached the building. "Help me God please save me."

The words tumbled from her mouth in a jumble, but she continued to scream them out in hopes they would attract someone. She hustled past the end of the building and turned left to follow it to what she hoped would eventually be the lobby. A wail ripped from her chest when her eyes fell on two men across the road by the corn. Her heart soared. One was wearing a uniform, and unless she was mistaken, he was law enforcement.

Jen began to wave her hand in the air, hoping to draw their attention long before reaching them. The two men glanced toward her. They appeared to be arguing, but she didn't care, happy to find more people. They could help run Orville off or, better yet, make sure to put him in the ground.

"Jesus, honey," a woman's voice said, freezing Jen in her tracks.

She turned to find a middle-aged woman standing in the parking lot. Jen's eyes slid to a girl she guessed was her daughter, peeking over her shoulder. She couldn't place her age, seeing anything from twelve years old to in her early twenties.

"Anna, go in and get some more water and a towel," the woman said.

The girl stepped back, her eyes locked onto Jen, until her heel struck the curb. Spinning, the girl rushed into the motel, stopping only once more to get a final look at Jen.

A shiver worked down Jen's back when their eyes met. *Something wrong with that one.* She shook her head, unsure why she thought that, but something in her gut said it was true.

"Oh, thank God," she slipped to her knees as the strength fled her limbs.

The woman hurried to her side and squatted down to wrap her arms around her. "It's gonna be all right."

"Now don't be making promises to strangers just yet," the man in the uniform growled as he marched towards the women.

"What do you mean?" the older woman asked as she rocked Jen in her arms.

"The season isn't over yet, and sacrifices must be made for all our sakes."

What does that mean? The question hovered in Jen's head. Laughter floated on the breeze, and it took her a moment to realize it didn't come from anyone she could see.

"What the fuck?" the other man whispered, disbelief overwhelming his voice.

Jen glanced across the road, gasping at The Scarecrow standing just above the ears of corn. It stared directly at her with round black circles that sparkled in the setting sunlight. Behind it, crows flew into the air until a long shadow cast over the road and began to creep towards them. Jen's breath caught as the shadow appeared to be a hand inching closer.

It stopped moving when Jen and the woman were completely covered by the shade.

"This one is mine," a raspy voice uttered. "She bears the mark of my disciple."

"What are—," the woman's question cut short as the sheriff grabbed Jen by the armpits and lifted her from the ground.

"You heard him," he said in a gruff voice, the emotion he tried to hide coming through anyway. "If he claims her, it's too late. Unless you want to take her place?"

The woman glanced away, her cheeks flushing red in shame.

Jen struggled to get free, but the sheriff gripped her tighter. "Enough," he barked as he turned to carry her towards the corn.

"Please," she begged, unsure why but suddenly terrified to come any closer to the field.

The sheriff carried her past the other man, who turned his head as if she would simply disappear from his mind if he could no longer see her.

This can't be happening. Did she escape one madman only to be found by a group of them? She kicked back with her foot, smiling at the satisfying crunch of her heel striking the sheriff's groin. His grip loosened, and she pulled free.

Jen grimaced at the pain jolting through her ankle as she landed on the ground. Without looking back, she bolted into the corn. *Nothing could be worse than these weirdoes, right?*

✳✳✳

A wave of pleasure flashed through Orville as Sheriff Pike crumpled to the ground. *Serves him right, she's mine to offer up.* He studied the others, using the corner of the motel to shield his bulk from their sight should they glance his way. The sun was lower now, but still, there was too much light to try and cross just yet.

"Whatcha doin'?" a voice asked from behind him.

Orville spun around, ready to charge at the speaker. A pretty girl leaned out of a window. Orville stared a moment before realizing it was the same window he had peeped through all those weeks ago. *Meaning this is the girl at the pond.* He stepped closer, issuing a hissing shushing noise. It wouldn't do to have the others drawn over here to investigate who the girl was speaking with.

"Quiet," he said in an exaggerated whisper. "I'm waiting to go to the corn, and I don't want the sheriff seein' me."

"Huh … is that why you wearin' that mask?" she asked, leaning further out to look around his large frame.

His eyes ran from her long hair, fixed into a sloppy ponytail, down the length of her neck, slowing to take in the swell of her breasts, exaggerated by her arched back, then moving to her waist, where the house blocked him from seeing more. *This is no girl.* Of that, he was sure; and yet, he couldn't place her age. At first, he would have guessed no older than thirteen or fourteen when she spoke, and his first glance added a few years to that estimate. Now as he stood closer, he wondered if she might be older still, possibly as old as he was.

A knowing smile bloomed on her lips, and she batted her eyes at him. He felt the blood rush to his face, and instead of just the heat of embarrassment, pain arrived as well. He desperately wanted to rip off the burlap, to relieve himself from the itchy, hot fabric, but instead, he leaned closer to the girl.

"You keep quiet or I'll come back and visit you one night," he growled.

The girl studied his masked face a moment. "I suspect from the shine in your right eye, you plan on payin' me a visit no matter what I do."

Orville straightened. She wasn't wrong, but it was her comment on his eye that grabbed his attention. His vision was still bathed in red, but, he realized, not so much from the left. He turned from the girl and moved to the corner. Everyone was now standing around the sheriff, who still lay on the ground. A number of crows appeared from the corn, flying to form a black wall of motion between them and his path to the corn. Without glancing back, Orville rushed across the road to find Jen.

CHAPTER FORTY-THREE

Jen walked in a crouch down a row, hoping the direction took her towards the main town and away from the motel. The last thing she needed was to run into those lunatics again. Sweat soaked through her dress, and for a brief moment, she thought of the cool cavern. Shaking her head, she chased those thoughts away. *I'll take every day in this heat rather than think about what he was planning for me down there.*

Her toe stubbed into a clump 'f raised earth, jerking her foot and aggravating her ankle. She bit her bottom lip and slumped to the ground. The dull ache began to intensify, and she pressed her palm into her lips, hoping to dampen the scream building in her chest.

"Are you all right, ma'am?" a gruff voice whispered.

Jen's eyes widened as panic washed over her. *They found me!*

She struggled to stand, but a hand fell on her shoulder to stop her. She glanced back and sighed. She was staring at a stranger. Opening her mouth to ask who he was, she paused when she recognized his uniform, the same one the sheriff wore.

"You're one of them," she spat out as she pulled away from his touch.

He wore a confused look before his eyes lit up in understanding. He squatted to be on eye level. "No, I'm not one of them. I'm trying to figure out who they are. Did they do this to you?"

"What? No ... I did this when I escaped from Orville," she said with a wave of her hand. "I just want to know what happened to Sam and get out of here."

"Then why are you scared of *them*?" By the look on her face, his hope of receiving treatment at the motel was becoming less and less of an option.

"They were trying to give me to ... someone," she finally said, not really sure *what* actually transpired, just that something did.

"What is your name?" he asked with a sigh, extending his hand. "I'm Deputy Boyle. You can call me Teddy."

She grabbed it and gave it a quick shake. "Jen. Are you okay?"

He pressed his hand against the gash on his forehead and offered a slight nod. "Just an accident. I was planning on getting help over at the motel, but sounds like we're on our own."

"I don't know about that, Deputy," Orville said with a giggle as he pushed through the stalks.

Anna watched the man run to the corn. She looked forward to their next interaction, but for now, she was limited in her choice of playthings. Slipping back into the room, she spun to face the mirror and studied her reflection with a wicked smile. She was filling out nicely, and soon she would be fully formed. *Just need a tiny boost.*

Anna strolled into the front of the motel, past the counter, and to the main lobby where Deputy Smite sat with his eyes closed. She stepped lightly until she stood next to him. She studied the hilt of the knife and the wound, visible through a tear in the man's shirt. Her tongue snaked out, trailing slowly across her bottom lip before turning upwards. She paused with it pressed against the middle of her upper lip, then sucked it back into her mouth.

A soft moan slipped past Smite's lips. His eyes fluttered open, blinking until they focused on Anna as she slid in front of him. She leaned forward, resting her hands on his knees. His eyes darted from her face to the opening of her shirt, where she knew he could see her breasts hanging. A bead of sweat formed above his right eye and ran down, getting caught in his thick eyebrow.

She pursed her lips together and leaned closer. The sweat dropped unexpectantly into his eye, and he gasped at the sting. Her hands slid up from his knees to stop on his thighs. He gripped the arms of the chair until they creaked. With wide eyes, she offered a soft moan before pulling herself up onto his lap. Her hands slid farther up until they rested on his chest.

She nodded to the knife. "I can help with that … and I can help with this." Her voice was a husky whisper as she squirmed on his growing erection. "Do … you … want … my … help?"

Smite's mouth hung slack. She shifted to her knees, slipping them beside his hips so she could straddle him. With her hands resting on his shoulders, she moved even closer, her lips just barely hovering over his. His eyes were wide, and she smiled as she saw his lustful desires overpower all his other senses. She ran her hand up to his cheek and leaned closer to press her lips against his.

He went rigid, trembling as if an electric current coursed 279hroughh his body. With her other hand, she gripped the hilt of the knife. He groaned into her mouth, anticipating the pain, she imagined. Her tongue slipped past his lips and swirled with his just when she pulled the knife free. His eyes rolled back, and he groaned once more. She let the knife drop to the floor with a clang and deepened the kiss, pressing her palm flat against the open wound.

Anna moaned as the current moved from her lips down her arm and back into Smite. His hands sprang up, grasping her breasts through her shirt and pressing the soft fabric against her erect nipples. She responded by rocking ever so slightly, rubbing her crotch against his erection. The energy flowing through the kiss increased, and Anna pulled her hand away from Smite's shoulder to reveal a pink, puckered scar.

Breaking off the kiss, she flung her head back as she let out tiny gasps of ecstasy. Her body was on fire, sending tingles throughout, but she knew she needed to stop. She pulled his hands from her chest, placing them in his lap as she scooted off the chair. She looked down at the deputy, aware that she stood taller than moments before. She reached out and touched his cheek lovingly.

"You are mine now," she purred. "You will answer my every call. Now sleep."

Smite's eyelids grew heavy, and in a moment, his head slumped forward, gentle snores announcing his compliance. Anna hurried back to the bathroom and stood once more in front of the mirror. She was a few inches taller, her arms and legs now longer as well.

Her skin was darker, as if she sat in the sun for too long, and her eyes shifted from brown to blue to green. Her hair, still in a ponytail, now hung farther down her back, and the color was no longer a dirty blonde but closer to caramel. She smiled at her reflection, noting her canines had lengthened and ended in points. Soon her maturation would be complete.

Anna clapped her hands together, giggling in excitement.

CHAPTER FORTY-FOUR

Boyle rolled to a stop. His jaw creaked as he opened and closed it. *Man packs a punch.* Orville stood a few feet away, towering over Jen, who now lay curled up in a shuddering heap. She didn't even try to escape when he told her to run. Boyle stood, his hand sliding to his holster. Drawing his weapon, he aimed at Orville's incredible center mass.

"What's with the bag?" he called out to get Orville's attention off the woman. "I mean, you weren't all that pretty before."

Orville's head jerked up, and Boyle recognized the hatred burning bright in his right eye. The hulking man clenched his hands into tight fists until blood dripped to the earth below. Jen's soft cries tugged at Boyle's heart. He had heard this sound many a time in the war; the sound of defeat, of complete surrender. *This girl's given up.* Sighing, he closed one eye to aim properly. *One way to fix that.*

A blur swept from the corn, pull'ng between the two men as Boyle pulled the trigger. Black feathers and blood splattered out as his bullet tore into one of the many crows that populated the area.

"And is that a fair fight?" a dry, rough voice said softly.

A black-gloved hand appeared from the stalks and grabbed the revolver, pulling it down and out of Boyle's hand. His gaze swept from the hand, up an arm, and to the stitched smile of The Scarecrow. The creature's dark stone eyes twinkled in what he could only assume was excitement. It tossed his gun across the row.

"If you defeat my disciple, you may take the girl and leave," it said, pointing to Orville. "But if you lose … you join the harvest."

Unsure what to say, even more unsure what was going on, Boyle found he only truly had one choice. He nodded and stepped away from the creature. A caw sounded from above. Afraid to remove his eyes from The Scarecrow or Orville, he ignored the bird, even after it repeated its call once more. A blur sped to the ground, and a hatchet bounced off the hard-packed dirt.

Orville sprang over Jen's prone body, rushing towards the weapon. Boyle weighed his options before barking out a curse and diving for the hatchet. The Scarecrow offered an amused chuckle as it stepped to Jen.

"Time is running out," it said, squatting next to the woman.

Boyle cried out as Orville slammed his foot down on his hand, pinning it to the ground inches short of the weapon. Orville scooped up the hatchet, leaning so all his weight came down on Boyle's hand. A loud crack filled his ears a moment before the flash of pain rode to his brain. Orville let loose a blast of laughter as the deputy screamed in agony.

"Serves you right," he spat out, raising his foot up to once more drive it down on any part of Boyle he could connect with.

Boyle rolled at the last minute, more out of instinct than anything else, and the boot slammed onto the dirt. Cradling his wounded hand, he scurried away from the towering man. If he was lucky, he might find his gun, otherwise, he knew he was going to be hard-pressed to stop them from doing what they wanted to the girl or himself.

The Scarecrow stood with Jen in its arms. It stepped over to Orville and presented her as if she were a present. "My poor child, what have they done to you?"

Orville only shook his head in answer as he took Jen.

The Scarecrow patted him on the shoulder before placing his hand against the large man's cheek. "I can offer you some relief in the form of distraction, but remember, you must return her to me in time or all is forfeit."

"Noooo," Boyle screamed as the hulking man carried her away, deeper into the corn.

Pike sat up. His groin ached, but he was pretty sure he'd live. Everyone save the girl stood around him. He took a few deep breaths and held his hand up. Robert grabbed it and pulled him to his feet. A blast of fresh pain in his groin tied a knot in his stomach. *Damn, she got me good.* He bent at the waist and took a few more breaths.

A shot sounded off in the corn.

Pike jerked straight with a groan. *Who the hell has a gun out there?*

"You folks best get inside," he said as he stepped to the edge of the field. "Deputy Smite is armed. Y'all are safer with him. Don't let nothin' in until I return."

Pike didn't look back as he entered the corn. He could hear voices ahead and was grateful the crows had quieted after that nonsense earlier. He drew his revolver and pulled the hammer back. He had no plans of getting caught unaware. They may have made a deal with this particular devil, but that didn't mean he trusted anything that had to do with the harvest.

His blood ran cold a' a man's agonized scream sounded up ahead. *Was that Boyle?* It would explain who fired the shot, but it made no sense. The man should be back at the office, not out here creeping around. He dropped down in a squat. He could see Orville carrying the woman away and The Scarecrow studying Boyle as he screamed in defiance.

"You may come out, Sheriff," The Scarecrow said without removing his gaze from the downed man.

Shit. Pike stepped into the row and glared at his deputy. "What part of *go to the office* did you not understand?"

"Had no choice," Boyle responded through clenched teeth. "Crows forced me off the road … sir."

Pike noted the heat in the man's voice. *This will never be over.* His head snapped in the direction Orville went as the woman's wail cut through the silence. The Scarecrow began to dance, simple steps at first but growing more intricate as the cry continued.

"Jesus Christ," Boyle shouted as he struggled to his feet. "Do something!"

The cry continued, only pausing for what Pike assumed were Orville's manipulations. It carried with it more disappointment and anguish than a dying town could contain, let alone a single person.

"I'm doing more than you can ever imagine," he said softly. His chest tightened as the mournful cry suddenly cut short.

"By sacrificing those prisoners, you mean?" Boyle stepped forward swinging his uninjured hand to point towards Orville's victim. "Or her?"

"You wouldn't understand," Pike said with a voice thick with emotion. "The question now is can you live with it?"

Boyle shuffled closer, trembling with rage. "Can I live with it? This is why they sent me here, to learn what you people are up to and why so many just fucking disappear."

"Figured as much," he said with a sigh. He raised his revolver and pulled the trigger. The bullet seemed to fly at Boyle in slow motion until it struck him directly on the deep gash at his temple. The man swayed back and forth, the look of shock on his face almost comical. He slid to his knees, blinking once before falling face-first onto the hard dirt.

Pike holstered his weapon and tipped his brim to The Scarecrow. "One more for your harvest, hoss."

"Will it be enough?" The Scarecrow hissed as it spread its arms wide.

"Is it ever?" Pike spat in the dirt next to Boyle's corpse. "How much of this do you actually need?"

The Scarecrow stepped over to the body and knelt down. It displayed the scythe to the sheriff, then jabbed the point into Boyle's neck and pulled the blade down until it reached the man's waist. It stuck its free hand into the body, rummaging around for a moment.

"Ahhh, this will do," it said, pulling out its gore-covered arm. In its hand was the man's heart, which seemed to shimmer in the dying light. "While they prefer to feast on the flesh of your kind on the other side, our master only requires the essence to complete the bargain."

Pike swallowed back the rising bile traveling up his esophagus. He refused to show any weakness in front of this monstrosity. He stepped to the deputy and squatted down to loop his arms through the man's armpits. Pike dragged the body away, keeping his eyes locked on The Scarecrow until the corn finally obscured it.

CHAPTER FORTY-FIVE

"Should I ask?" Pike asked, pointing towards Smite's now healed shoulder.

A painful grimace crossed the man's face, and he finally offered a simple shrug.

Pike nodded. *Some things are best forgotten.* If push came to shove, he'd put his money on the Tanners' girl, but he wasn't sure how to even begin to explain it. A problem for another day, he guessed.

They dropped Boyle's body off at Orville's place after they left the motel. He glanced at the report on his desk and smiled. *Says here we find it tomorrow around nine; plenty of time to get home and see the family and celebrate another successful harvest season.* With The Scarecrow finally claiming Orville, they met the quota on time once again. He'd let the town leadership know tomorrow there would be no visit this year.

At least something went right. He shuddered at the memory of his first year and The Scarecrow's reaction to them being short on the quota. He'd promised himself to never let it happen on his watch. *So far, so good.*

"We're going to be short-handed for a little bit," he said as he stood. "If you don't mind, I'll head home for a bit and relieve you in say … three hours?"

Smite nodded and waved, turning his attention back to the stack of reports he was working on. "See you then."

✳✳✳

Robert lay in bed, wide awake. He stared at the ceiling and prayed to a God he wasn't sure would listen to him. They made a mistake in bringing her back. He saw that now. The price was too high, and more importantly, whatever The Pale Man delivered wasn't his daughter.

Ruth woke with a start and rolled over.

"Robert, you awake?"

He fought the urge to lie, to pretend he slept so he could ignore his wife.

"Yep."

"I'm sorry," she whispered, pressing herself tight against his side. She hugged him for a moment. "We shouldn't have done it. I see that now."

"Yep."

"He came to me … in my dream," she said in a way that sounded like it was possibly all a lie. But he knew she spoke the truth since he also received a visit. "He said the harvest is short one. Said we had to choose who it would be … said it could be her. He'd take her back."

They lay quietly in the dark, each other's ragged breaths the only sound. Robert didn't know what to say. He couldn't harm his daughter or his wife. *But could you stand aside and let it happen?* He was pretty sure he could but instead opened his mouth to tell her he would give himself to The Pale Man.

Before he could speak, Ruth said, "I'll do it. I'll take her out to the corn and hand her to that … that thing."

Robert slammed his mouth closed, his teeth clicking together loudly. He nodded, unable to speak. Ruth kissed his cheek and rose from the bed. She slipped a thin cotton robe over her nightgown and hurried from the room.

In his mind, Robert played out his wife waking their daughter, convincing her to get up, and taking her through the corn to The Scarecrow's perch. So much death in three short weeks, and the cherry on top was his daughter served back to the one that made her return possible. His eye's shined with tears as he remembered how she was before the accident. Should he try the prayer again?

The bedroom door swung open. Robert continued to stare at the ceiling. He listened to her drop the robe on the floor and sigh as she crawled into bed. The bedsprings creaked, and his breath caught as she snuggled up tight against his side. She kissed him on the cheek, her hot breath tickling the skin. A single tear escaped from the corner of Robert's eye and rolled down his face.

DONN, TX 1926

"Why, Daddy, ain't ya happy to see me?"

The Shadow Within

"Eric Butler crossed a bold line in this book, and I loved it." – Sea Caummisar, author of the Raised By A Killer series.

Centuries ago, the native people imprisoned a spirit of pure evil and unending hunger.

Thirteen years ago, an eight-year-old boy woke the darkness. It grows in strength every day, and now that the boy is a man, adept in terror and violence, the darkness hopes to finally break free.

And here Jill thought the scariest thing on this vacation was going to be spending the week with her boyfriend's kids.

THE POPE LICK MASSACRE

There are two types of people in Jefferson County: those who know the legend of the Pope Lick Monster and those who believe it. Before the night is over, Sam will have no choice but to join the believers.

Since their mother's death, Sam's sole focus has been taking care of her younger brother, Kenny. Now Kenny's Scout troop is missing, having never returned from the woods around Pope Lick. Sam gathers a group of friends to search for the boys and their Scoutmaster. With each step, they get closer to discovering the scouts aren't the only ones in the woods this night.

"The Pope Lick Massacre is a bold, brutal horror story that'll remain in your mind long after you read it. This book is not for the faint of heart." –Independent Book Review

The Ephraim Godwin Chronicles
The Sins of the Past

Once an ancient race of supreme beings ruled over the earth. Banished by the light centuries ago, one has returned. With the help of its disciples, it desires to plunge the world into a new age of darkness and horror.

Ephraim Godwin is searching for the truth about his family's disappearance. After conventional ways failed, he turned to the world of spiritualism, only to discover it filled with charlatans and tricksters. As a known skeptic, Ephraim fights to shine a light on those who prey upon others as he searches for the truth.

As Ephraim attends another séance, he discovers not everyone is a fraud and is drawn deeper into the world of the supernatural. With the help of noted spiritualist Zona Whitlock and famed explorer Doctor Livingstone, he hopes to stop this evil from consuming the world.

There's Something In The Water
Expanded Edition

All Kurt Reedy needed for his lakeside development project to go through was the land owned by Chuck Miller. The only problem was Miller refused to sell his family's legacy. In the past, Reedy may have resorted to violence to get his way, but he was a legit businessman now.

Running out of time, he is forced to think outside the box. In his haste, he doesn't do the proper research, and now there's something in the water.

Something territorial.

Something hungry.

Kiss Me Where It Smells Funny

Alex has a crush on the new Teacher's assistant, and he's finally worked up the nerve to approach her.

Too bad she's crossed the University's star player, and Duncan Shaw has no choice but to make her disappear.

He plans to lay the blame on the local urban legend, but tonight he just might learn that some legends are real.

ABOUT THE AUTHOR

Eric Butler does the daily bidding of three huskies, but somehow finds time to write horror fiction. With a twenty-year marriage and a grown son by his side, he won't be running out of material any time soon. His works include *The Pope Lick Massacre*, *The Rest Stop*, and *The Shadow Within*, and his stories can be found in countless anthologies. Eric and his family call North Richland Hills, Texas their home.

READ INDIE HORROR
AND FEED A HUSKY

www.ingramcontent.com/pod-product-compliance
Lightning Source LLC
Chambersburg PA
CBHW021213250626
47155CB00008B/2793